A HEAVEN ON EARTH

Phyllis sat down looking very serious.

"There be all manner of strange things in this old world, especially here in the West Country, that cannot be accounted for, and I'm sure if she does come to you again, Miss Aurora, you will know just what to do."

Aurora smiled.

"Thank you Phyllis, I am sure you are right, that is just what Mama would have said."

She paused for a moment to gaze out of the window at the garden, which was still bathed in winter sunlight.

"What day is it, Phyllis?" she asked. "I have lost all count of time, what with being ill."

"It be the sixth of January today, miss, the last day of Christmas."

Aurora sat back and recounted all the extraordinary things that had happened to her since her return home on Christmas Eve.

And now the New Year was already six days old, and there was no knowing what the coming months might bring.

She thought of the Earl, recalling how animated and happy he had appeared as he rode with them to Hadleigh Hall through the snow.

And the thrill that had run over her body when he had invited her to dine with him.

Could it really be the case that she would never feel that wonderful sensation ever again?

THE BARBARA CARTLAND PINK COLLECTION

Titles in this series

A HEAVEN ON EARTH

BARBARA CARTLAND

Barbaracartland.com Ltd

THE BARBARA CARTLAND PINK COLLECTION

Barbara Cartland was the most prolific bestselling author in the history of the world. She was frequently in the Guinness Book of Records for writing more books in a year than any other living author. In fact her most amazing literary feat was when her publishers asked for more Barbara Cartland romances, she doubled her output from 10 books a year to over 20 books a year, when she was 77.

She went on writing continuously at this rate for 20 years and wrote her last book at the age of 97, thus completing 400 books between the ages of 77 and 97.

Her publishers finally could not keep up with this phenomenal output, so at her death she left 160 unpublished manuscripts, something again that no other author has ever achieved.

Now the exciting news is that these 160 original unpublished Barbara Cartland books are already being published and by Barbaracartland.com exclusively on the internet, as the international web is the best possible way of reaching so many Barbara Cartland readers around the world.

The 160 books are published monthly and will be numbered in sequence.

The series is called the Pink Collection as a tribute to Barbara Cartland whose favourite colour was pink and it became very much her trademark over the years.

The Barbara Cartland Pink Collection is published only on the internet. Log on to www.barbaracartland.com to find out how you can purchase the books monthly as they are published, and take out a subscription that will ensure that all subsequent editions are delivered to you by mail order to your home.

NEW

Barbaracartland.com is proud to announce the publication of ten new Audio Books for the first time as CDs. They are favourite Barbara Cartland stories read by well-known actors and actresses and each story extends to 4 or 5 CDs. The Audio Books are as follows:

The Patient Bridegroom	The Passion and the Flower
A Challenge of Hearts	Little White Doves of Love
A Train to Love	The Prince and the Pekinese
The Unbroken Dream	A King in Love
The Cruel Count	A Sign of Love

More Audio Books will be published in the future and the above titles can be purchased by logging on to the website www.barbaracartland.com or please write to the address below.

If you do not have access to a computer, you can write for information about the Barbara Cartland Pink Collection and the Barbara Cartland Audio Books to the following address:

Barbara Cartland.com Ltd., Camfield Place,
Hatfield, Hertfordshire AL9 6JE, United Kingdom.

Telephone: +44 (0)1707 642629
Fax: +44 (0)1707 663041

THE LATE DAME BARBARA CARTLAND

Barbara Cartland who sadly died in May 2000 at the age of nearly 99 was the world's most famous romantic novelist who wrote 723 books in her lifetime with worldwide sales of over 1 billion copies and her books were translated into 36 different languages.

As well as romantic novels, she wrote historical biographies, 6 autobiographies, theatrical plays, books of advice on life, love, vitamins and cookery. She also found time to be a political speaker and television and radio personality.

She wrote her first book at the age of 21 and this was called *Jigsaw*. It became an immediate bestseller and sold 100,000 copies in hardback and was translated into 6 different languages. She wrote continuously throughout her life, writing bestsellers for an astonishing 76 years. Her books have always been immensely popular in the United States, where in 1976 her current books were at numbers 1 & 2 in the B. Dalton bestsellers list, a feat never achieved before or since by any author.

Barbara Cartland became a legend in her own lifetime and will be best remembered for her wonderful romantic novels, so loved by her millions of readers throughout the world.

Her books will always be treasured for their moral message, her pure and innocent heroines, her good looking and dashing heroes and above all her belief that the power of love is more important than anything else in everyone's life.

"Many times I have been asked, 'does love really make the world go round, Barbara?' and I always reply, 'it does for me. How about you?'"

Barbara Cartland

CHAPTER ONE
1877

"I think we are almost there! We've just turned off the road!" Aurora cried, as the carriage swung to the right, lurching and swaying.

"I know that bump in the drive so well. I thought Papa would have fixed it by now."

She leapt up in her excitement and peered through the carriage window, but it was very steamed up on this icy December day, so she then pulled it open and cold foggy air came flooding in.

"Ouch!" called out Phyllis, her maid, shivering as she huddled to the corner of the seat. "You'll surely freeze us both to death, Miss Aurora!"

Aurora laughed and pulled up the fur-lined hood of her cloak round her ears.

"Just let me have the first glimpse of Hadleigh Hall, and then I'll shut the window," she replied and she leaned out and looked longingly up the drive ahead of them.

It was almost a mile from the road to the Hall and the tall trees Aurora's great-grandfather had planted hid the rolling fields and moors from view.

The carriage rolled swiftly forward, pulled by two powerful grey horses that raced on, eager to return to the stables for their teatime feed.

Aurora gasped in delight as a graceful deer flitted out from the trees and bounded across the drive.

Then she felt her heart melt with joy as she saw the twinkling lights of Hadleigh Hall appear around the bend.

The twisting chimneys and long sloping roof of the old building were silvery with frost and the lights from the windows looked magical through the mist.

"It's wonderful to be back," sighed Aurora, taking pity on Phyllis and shutting the window. "I cannot believe that I have been away for four whole months."

"Oh, Miss Aurora," came in Phyllis. "I can't wait for a nice cup of tea after all that nasty French coffee."

"I'm so sorry, Phyllis, I know how much you hated being stuck in France, but what would I have done at the Finishing School without you?"

She thought of the imposing square building on the Paris boulevard with its endless polished floors and hard beds for the pupils and the strict teachers who taught her so much about etiquette and manners.

When Aurora had arrived in France, she spoke only a few words of the language and she had to work so hard at her French as well as her drawing and music to satisfy the high standards of the Finishing School.

It had been such a comfort to have Phyllis with her to chat to in the mornings and after 'lights out'.

She did not have to struggle to explain to Phyllis about how she wanted her clothes and her hair to look, as she would have had to do if she had been assigned one of the severe French maids who had waited on the other girls.

The carriage then came to a sudden stop, the wheels crunching over the gravel and after a moment Thomas, the coachman, opened the door.

Aurora pulled her long cloak around her and taking Thomas's hand swung herself down to the ground.

"Merry Christmas!"

She looked up to see Lady Hartnell, her stepmother, sweep gracefully down the front steps, her grey hair piled high on her head and her purple silk skirts rustling.

Aurora stood on tiptoe to kiss her stepmother and as she did so, she could not but notice that the purple of her dress was a little too bright and not quite what the elegant Frenchwomen she had been living with for the last months would have chosen.

"Where is Papa?" enquired Aurora, as she followed Lady Hartnell into the marble-floored hall.

"He is resting, my dear. He will see you when he comes down for dinner. Perhaps you should now go and freshen up, you have had a very long journey."

She put on her *pince-nez* to scrutinise Aurora's face closely, making her feel uncomfortable as she realised that her face must be red and shiny with her hair in a mess.

The fire was aglow in her bedroom with candles on the dressing table and as soon as the footmen had put down her luggage, Aurora rang the bell for the kitchen maid to bring her tea and toast.

"I know it's not long for dinner, but I can't wait," Aurora muttered, as Phyllis helped her out of her cloak and dress and sat her in front of the mirror to brush the tangles out of her long auburn hair.

"Nor me, miss. I'm proper parched. My, look how long your hair has grown since we was last here."

Aurora gazed at her reflection and took in her thick auburn curls framing her heart-shaped face and large blue eyes.

There was indeed something different about her and despite the warm childish flush on her cheeks, she realised that the last time she had looked in this mirror, she was still a child and now she was a woman and the thought made her feel strangely excited.

"Put my hair up nicely please, Phyllis?" she asked. "I want to look my best for Papa."

There was a knock on the door and the maid came bustling in with a tray jingling with cups and a huge china teapot and a large silver cover over a plate of hot toast.

"Sit still now or it will never be done," said Phyllis, as she twisted Aurora's glossy hair into an intricate crown of plaits – the very latest French style.

Aurora turned to face forwards again so that Phyllis could go to work with her comb and hairpins, pinning long plaits up in a graceful knot at the back of her head.

It was so good to be home again and in her familiar bedroom with its flowered chintz curtains and pretty white chinaware on the washstand, but Aurora just could not help wishing for something a little bit more exciting.

Dinner with her Papa and 'Mama', as Lady Hartnell insisted on being called, even though she was not Aurora's real mother, would be a quiet affair.

Papa would ask endless questions about the school in France with Lady Hartnell adding in her own comments, when she was not moaning about the food and criticising the servants waiting at table.

Aurora sighed as she thought of the evening ahead, but what a contrast it would be to the crowd of chattering girls she had left behind in France.

At that moment she realised that the time ahead was going to be a quiet and lonely one for her.

Of course, there was always dear Phyllis, who was always happy to talk away.

Phyllis had known Aurora since she was a baby and would probably still be around at Hadleigh Hall when she was old with her beautiful auburn curls turned white.

"There you are Miss Aurora. You're done and very lovely you are too, prettier than any of them mademoiselles with all their airs and graces!"

Phyllis then brought over the big white bowl from the washstand and started sponging down Aurora's neck and arms, which was very refreshing after the long journey.

When she had finished, Aurora told her to go and help herself to tea and toast.

"Aren't you havin' any?" asked Phyllis, lifting the silver cover and sniffing the piping hot toast underneath.

"I don't feel hungry after all."

Aurora wanted to be quiet for a moment and sip her tea, looking at her reflection in front of the long mirror.

The longing for something exciting to happen was growing stronger inside her and she knew that although she might miss all the fun of schoolgirl chatter about hairstyles and petticoats, there was no going back.

'I am a woman now,' she whispered to herself, 'and a woman needs a man beside her to look after her. I would like to meet someone who cares about me as much as Papa does, but who is there just for me.'

She felt her face become warm at the thought and sure enough, she could see from her reflection that she had gone pink.

"Whatever you be a-dreamin' about, Miss Aurora, you'd better stop," murmured Phyllis, finishing a mouthful of toast and wiping her hands carefully, before she lifted a beautiful green silk dress from the bed.

"Thank you, Phyllis," muttered Aurora, glancing at the clock on the mantelpiece her Papa had given her for her twelfth birthday. "It's nearly time for dinner, I know."

The dress was a perfect fit and was complemented by touches of pale green lace at the shoulders and over the

5

fashionable bustle at the back that made Aurora look even more womanly and grown-up.

"Here, Miss Aurora – "

Phyllis ran over to the windowsill, where a tall red-flowered geranium stood proudly in a china pot and pulled off some of the bright red petals.

She rubbed the petals between her fingers and then went to rub the colour onto Aurora's lips and cheeks.

"No!" cried Aurora, suddenly feeling embarrassed. "I don't think Papa would approve."

"Why, all girls do it! They used to do it even when I was a girl. I don't see no harm in it, miss."

"Not tonight,"

Aurora pushed Phyllis gently away, feeling sad that there would be no one at the dinner who would appreciate her subtle natural colouring.

Suddenly there was loud booming crash.

It was Treginnis, the butler, beating the gong.

Aurora smoothed down her green skirts and took a final look in the mirror before swishing down the staircase to take her place at the dinner table.

The dining room was panelled in dark shining oak that reflected the light from the candles burning brightly all the way along the ancient refectory table.

It was a very long table for just three people.

Lord Hartnell, frail and white-haired, made his way with tottering steps to its head and Lady Hartnell, looking resplendent in a purple dress which was now augmented by a purple feather in her hair, marched to sit opposite him at the other end.

Aurora was sitting half-way between them – in the middle of one of the long sides of the table and had to turn her head from side to side as they spoke to her.

"It is so good to have you home at last, my dear," intoned her father, his voice sounding thin and reedy as he smiled at Aurora.

"Yes, indeed," agreed Lady Hartnell with a frown. "Treginnis, you may serve the soup."

Treginnis started to make his way slowly about the table, pouring a little soup into each of their plates.

When they had all been served and Aurora had seen her father taste the soup, she picked up her own spoon, but just as she would put it to her lips, Lady Hartnell spoke,

"Such an unusual dress, Aurora. I cannot help but think it rather an unwise choice for so young a girl."

Aurora attempted to explain to her that the dress had come from one of the very best dressmakers in Paris and Madame Perrier, the Headmistress, had suggested that the style was the very latest and most suitable for her.

"And the colour! Awful! Reminds me of pea soup. If one must have colour, let it be bright."

Lady Hartnell raised her own spoon to her mouth.

"Madame Perrier told me that this exact shade of green would go very well with auburn hair," added Aurora.

She was about to explain Madame Perrier's opinion that bright shades were too strong for young girls to wear.

But Lady Hartnell had dropped her spoon into her bowl with a crash and gone bright red in the face.

"Treginnis!" she roared. "This soup is *cold*!"

The butler flustered around collecting the plates to return them and the soup tureen to the kitchen.

Aurora felt sorry for him, as he looked much older since the last time she had seen him and his black coat was too tight for him now and was straining at the buttons.

'How mean of my stepmother not to buy him a new coat,' thought Aurora, 'he has been with the family for as long as I can remember and he has always served us well.'

Lady Hartnell seemed a bit calmer now that she had made a fuss and she turned to Aurora with a frosty smile.

"I am sure, my dear, that you will have made more suitable choices for the other dresses you bought in Paris?"

Aurora felt her face redden and she hoped it did not show in the candlelight.

The green dress had been most expensive and had taken nearly all her clothes allowance, but Madame Perrier had advised her that it was more elegant to have one really good dress than several cheaper and less stylish outfits.

Lady Hartnell raised one long arm and stroked the purple sleeve of her dress.

"I, of course, have an excellent arrangement with my dressmaker," she boasted. "By making a judicious and economical choice of fabric, I was able to have two dresses for the price of one, this lovely heliotrope silk and also the crimson, which you like so much, Henry."

She raised her eyebrows and gazed down the table at Lord Hartnell, who was looking longingly at the empty plate in front of him.

Aurora was relieved as it seemed that Lady Hartnell had now stopped paying so much attention to her.

When she did find out that Aurora had spent most of her allowance on one dress, there was going to be *trouble*.

Treginnis entered again with the soup tureen.

"Cook has reheated the soup, my Lady," he said in a low voice.

"Oh, no, I don't think so. The time has passed for soup, Treginnis. Let's have the fish course. *Immediately!*"

The old butler hesitated, balancing the heavy tureen and then turned and headed back to the kitchen.

'Just how can she be so unkind?' mused Aurora. 'Treginnis is only doing what she has asked him to and she hasn't even said a word of thanks to him.'

Aurora's father was clearly feeling the same way, as he looked up and smiled at the old butler.

"Thanks very much, Treginnis, the fish course will be most welcome. I really am very hungry tonight."

'Poor Papa,' thought Aurora, 'he wants everyone to be happy and that's not easy to achieve, especially with someone like Lady Hartnell.'

Lord Hartnell turned his smile on his daughter.

"I do hope you have managed to find some lovely dresses in Paris, my dear, you may find yourself in need of them in the coming days."

"Why, Papa?"

Aurora suddenly felt a little thrill of anticipation.

"We have a new neighbour. We must ask him for dinner one night so he can make your acquaintance."

Aurora's heart gave a jump and she looked at the empty place on the other side of the polished oak table.

She could picture a tall handsome man sitting there gazing expectantly into her eyes.

"Oh, that's brought the roses to your cheeks. You must find it very dull here with just the two of us."

"Oh, no Papa, of course not," cried Aurora, but she could not keep the excitement from her voice.

The kitchen door swung open again and Treginnis entered bearing a whole salmon on a large plate, which he carried over to Lady Hartnell.

"Then who is it, Papa?" whispered Aurora, as her stepmother carved the fish. "Who is our new neighbour?"

"There is a newcomer at Elton Hall," he replied in a whisper as well. *"Lord Moreton!"*

Aurora wanted to jump up from the table and run around the room like a child, but, of course, being a young woman now she had to stay quietly in her seat.

She looked at her father with glowing eyes, longing to ask him all about Lord Moreton – if he was young and good-looking as she imagined him to be.

"I suppose this is edible," Lady Hartnell was saying in a loud voice, as she attacked a piece of salmon with her silver fork. "You may serve his Lordship, Treginnis."

It was agony for Aurora to wait as her father and stepmother slowly ate, but she had been well brought up at the French Finishing School and so she knew better than to speak before she was spoken to.

"Have you told her, Henry?" asked Lady Hartnell at last, removing a bone from between her teeth. "I thought I heard you muttering away just then."

"I have, my dear, and I may say she responded just as I would have hoped."

"Any young girl would be delighted, I am sure, to hear that such a wealthy and eligible bachelor has moved into the neighbourhood. Do finish your salmon, Aurora, we are ready for the next course."

Aurora could hardly eat even a morsel, she was so bursting with questions about Lord Moreton.

It seemed an extraordinary coincidence that she had been wishing for someone to come into her life, and there he was, about to appear, and perhaps become that special one she really longed for.

"Well, Aurora," suggested her Papa. "What would you say if I were to invite our new neighbour to dine with us on Boxing Day?"

Aurora stammered as she tried to find her words.

"That would – would be – most – "

Lord Hartnell laughed, shaking his grey head.

"Oh, Aurora, I am happy for you. I have a feeling things here at home are not going to be so dull after all."

Treginnis was bringing in the meat course with the aid of a young kitchen maid.

Under cover of the bustle of serving and tasting at Lady Hartnell's end of the table, Aurora was able to speak privately to her father.

"Papa, Papa, tell me. What is Lord Moreton like?"

"Now then, Aurora. You know what they say about curiosity. It killed the cat," he chuckled to himself.

"Papa!"

Aurora reached out to catch her father's hand, but he was too far away from her at the head of the table.

"He is a most delightful fellow. Most charming. I know you are going to like him very much."

"Yes," whispered Aurora. "I think I am."

"And perhaps more importantly, dear Aurora, he is a very wealthy man. Charm is all very well, but even the most delightful improves with the addition of great riches!"

He nodded gravely and gave her a serious look.

"Of course, Papa,"

Aurora closed her eyes for a moment.

The excitement was too much to bear, as not only was Lord Moreton handsome and polite and charming, but he was also rich and would never never be angry if Aurora spent all her clothes allowance on one lovely dress.

"What are you thinking about, my dear?"

"It seems just too good to be true."

"Yes, yes, exactly," muttered Lord Hartnell with a smile, as Treginnis served him with beef and vegetables.

"What secrets are you sharing down at that end of the table?" growled Lady Hartnell with a roguish gleam in her eye, as she raised her wine glass to her lips.

Aurora had noticed many times that her stepmother became so much more cheerful after a couple of glasses of wine, although if she had too many glasses, it could have the opposite effect.

"The charming Lord Moreton, of course!" replied Aurora's Papa, raising his glass to his wife.

"*Our* charming Lord Moreton, if I might call him that," laughed Lady Hartnell and emptied her glass.

"What does she mean, Papa," asked Aurora.

"Why, Aurora. My dearest Charlotte is just looking ahead to the happy day when you and Lord Moreton are joined together in Holy Matrimony!"

"But I haven't even met him!" exclaimed Aurora, feeling somewhat coy that her stepmother had noticed how excited she was and how eager to meet this wonderful man.

"No, but I must tell you that Lord Moreton is now the owner of Elton Manor estate, which adjoins our own lands and I need hardly add that if you were to be married to him – why, our two estates would be united as one."

And both he and her stepmother raised their glasses for another toast, laughing and winking at each other.

"Just think, my lovely daughter, how lucky you are – and how happy you will make me."

Aurora now could not touch a mouthful of the food in front of her.

Suddenly her life was about to change.

She was soon to meet this handsome wealthy man who would love her and marry her and she would have a beautiful house all of her own at Elton Manor, but still be close to home and to her dear Papa.

After dinner Aurora made her way up to her room.

Her head was spinning and her heart was pounding.

"Oh, Phyllis," she cried, as her maid helped her out of the green silk frock. "I am so excited, I am not going to be able to sleep a wink."

"I know it's Christmas Eve, miss, but you ain't six years old no more, Miss Aurora. You'll need your rest or you'll be tired from all them festivities."

"But listen to this, Phyllis – "

She then told her all about Lord Moreton and her father's plans for her marriage.

Phyllis was listening quietly as she turned down the bedcovers and laid out Aurora's nightgown.

"Well, Miss Aurora," she commented, when Aurora had finished. "I would have you remember there's *many* a slip twixt the cup and the lip!"

As Aurora lay in her bed gazing at the moonlight shining brightly through the chintz curtains, she wondered what Phyllis could have meant.

Lord Moreton was coming to Hadleigh Hall the day after tomorrow and the moment she saw him she just knew that her life would change forever.

She would be happy – Papa would be happy – what could possibly go wrong?

CHAPTER TWO

Aurora awoke on Boxing Day to a cold white light streaming in through her bedroom window and to hear the parlour maid rattling in the fireplace as she raked over the ashes and laid a new fire.

"It be a cold one, Miss Aurora," Phyllis remarked, as she placed a jug of hot water on the washstand.

Aurora threw off her covers and sat up to look out of the window.

Fog lay over all the lawns and gardens of Hadleigh Hall and everything bore a coating of crisp white frost.

"How is Papa this morning?" she asked Phyllis.

Her father had retired early to his bed on Christmas Day, saying that he felt tired and unwell after too much festivity, although in her opinion the day had in fact been very quiet.

Just herself, her Papa and her stepmother opening presents and eating mountains of delicious Christmas fare.

"He's still sleeping, miss, and your stepmother says he will not be down for breakfast."

"I shall go and see him later. Do you think that I might have breakfast in my room today?"

The thought of the long empty dining room on such a chilly morning was not a welcoming one.

"I was just going to suggest that very same thing," said Phyllis. "I should make the most of that water while it's still hot," and she disappeared off to the kitchen.

Aurora tucked herself under the covers once again and leaned back against the soft feather pillows to look at her presents that were piled up on the table by the bed.

She had never had so many Christmas presents.

She reached out to fondle a pair of white buttoned kid gloves, a pair of green dancing pumps and a pale blue silk dress.

The blue dress was not quite what she would have chosen for herself, it was more her stepmother's taste.

And she knew the colour was not very flattering to her complexion and auburn hair, but the silk it was made from was lovely and it was by far the finest dress she had ever been given.

Her Papa had given her a present of a beautiful pair of green earrings that suited her perfectly and she felt very happy as she turned them to catch the light.

She knew that he would have given a lot of thought to choosing them and that she would love them.

As soon as she had finished breakfast, she dressed herself warmly and putting on her thickest cloak, set out to take a walk around the shrubbery.

The branches of the trees looked magical with their sparkling decorations of frost, and, as she walked, the sun broke through and the fog began to lift, just as if the winter weather was in sympathy with her own joyful feelings.

'*Tonight* I am going to meet Lord Moreton,' she told herself again, 'and if I like him, we will be engaged.'

She wondered what Lord Moreton would look like, if he would be fair or dark and she hoped he would be tall and handsome and interesting to talk to.

But of course he would be, if her dear Papa thought that he might be a suitable match for her!

She wished for a moment that she was still at her Finishing School and could tell all her friends that she was about to be engaged, as this was the dearest hope and the favourite subject of conversation with the girls.

She could have wandered through the shrubbery all morning happily dreaming about Lord Moreton.

But the winter sun was now beginning to melt the glittering frost crystals and Aurora knew that it was time to return to the Hall and see if her Papa was awake and able to speak to her.

Lord Hartnell was sitting in a chair by the fire in his bedroom wrapped in a long velvet robe.

He was looking pale and tired and Aurora thought he seemed much older than when she had gone to France.

"Thank you, dear Papa, for the beautiful earrings. I do so love them," she said, touching her father's cold hand.

"I am so glad you like them," he smiled, "and there is a special reason for them as you will discover later."

Aurora longed to ask him what he meant, but then the white-haired old man waved her away gently.

"Off you go, my dear. I am very tired and I need to recover myself before tonight."

"Papa. Is all well with you? Is there anything I can do for you?"

"All is very well. I am so proud of you, my dearest daughter, and I have a distinct feeling that I am about to become even more so. But now I must ask you to leave me and I will see you at dinner."

Aurora left but she could not escape a slight feeling of anxiety about her father. He looked ill and fragile and she could never remember him staying in his room like this for so long.

'If I was my stepmother,' she thought to herself, 'I would want to be with him when he is not well and keep him company and I would try to lift his spirits and to make him feel better. Surely that is why people get married, to console each other and look after each other.'

But Lady Hartnell had her own way of doing things and Papa seemed to love her for all her forthrightness and lack of sympathy so perhaps he is happily married after all.

Aurora knew that the part she had to play was that of a dutiful, obedient and loving daughter.

'I must do my best to make him proud of me.'

She went to her room to go through her things with Phyllis so that all was ready for the evening.

*

Hadleigh Hall was ablaze with bright candles as the servants bustled around the dining room preparing the table for the evening's festivities.

Aurora was amazed to see whole bunches of grapes apparently growing from huge vases on the table and every other kind of fruit arranged in big silver dishes.

There were white flowers and bunches of greenery everywhere and she thought that she had never seen the dining room at Hadleigh Hall looking so resplendent.

If only she could wear her green dress!

She would look just perfect seated at the green-and-white table, but Lady Hartnell had come into her room that afternoon and found the dress laid out on the bed ready for Aurora to wear – and she had tossed it onto the floor.

"Ungrateful girl!" she had hissed. "What are you thinking of? Where is the Christmas gift from your father and myself? Surely that is more suitable for you to wear than this French frippery!"

Phyllis had quickly snatched the green dress from the floor and scurried away to hang it up.

"I thought perhaps – the green dress might be more suitable for tonight – " Aurora had stammered.

"Well – you thought wrong, young lady!" snorted Lady Hartnell. "Green indeed! Far too sophisticated for a girl like yourself. Whatever would Lord Moreton think of us? A nice innocent girlish blue would be perfect."

And she strode haughtily out of Aurora's bedroom, sweeping her silk train behind her.

"But what about Papa's earrings?" Aurora asked Phyllis, who was now laying out the pale blue silk on the bed. "I really ought to wear them or he will be hurt, but they are green – look here, these stones are emeralds – and they won't look at all right with blue."

Phyllis shook her head doubtfully and picked up the earrings, holding them up to Aurora's ears.

"I don't rightly know what to say, miss. They look just perfect on you, but they surely won't go with all that blue. *'Blue and green should ne'er be seen'*, that's what my old grandma told me."

"I've heard that saying too, Phyllis. Blue and green are meant to be unlucky together, aren't they? But I can't hurt Papa. I will just have to make the best of it."

As Aurora was finishing her dressing, she heard the rush of carriage wheels on the drive below her window and then the sound of loud voices talking and laughing.

She knew that Lord Moreton had just arrived.

'I won't peep out of the window,' she told herself, even though she was longing to do so. 'I want us both to see each other for the very first time when we meet in the drawing room!'

Phyllis hooked her carefully into the pale blue silk.

"It ain't so bad, Miss Aurora. It would have looked more right on Lady Hartnell when she was your age, her bein' fair-haired, but you don't look too bad at all."

Aurora had to agree when she saw her reflection in the mirror.

18

Pale blue was certainly not the best colour for her complexion, but it was a good colour for a young girl to wear and she looked fresh and pretty for Christmas.

But as she fixed the emerald clips onto her ears she felt uncomfortable.

She wanted to feel just perfect for this very special dinner, and she knew that those green stones did not look right next to the dress.

'I really cannot hurt Papa's feelings,' she reflected, 'he will not mind what I wear, but he would be very hurt if he thought I did not appreciate his beautiful gift.'

She did so want to look and feel absolutely perfect for the moment when Lord Moreton and she first laid eyes on each other.

So it was with a sad heart that she swept down the staircase and made her way towards the distant sound of voices in the drawing room.

'Oh, but perhaps I need not have worried so much,' she thought as she stood in the doorway, 'something has gone wrong and he is not here after all.'

Her stepmother was sitting on a long sofa with her scarlet skirts spread all around her.

Her Papa was standing near the fireplace, drinking sherry and conversing with a large man in a tight blue coat.

As she watched from the door, the man threw back ¹ and gave a roar of hearty laughter, which ended in ˙ˢ if he had run out of breath.

˙ᵉ?

ˀny of their tenant farmers, nor ,ᵉ of her father's neighbours.

ᵉ room and looked around to see ᴜng and handsome suitor she had ⅃ to meeting was hiding somewhere ، else in the room.

19

"Aurora, my dear!"

Her father approached her, eyes twinkling under his bushy white eyebrows,

"Allow me to introduce my dearest daughter," he continued, turning towards the large man in the blue coat and drawing him forward.

The man stepped forward and bowed, and as he did so, Aurora noticed that he had a large bald patch on top of his head that he had obviously tried to disguise by combing his straggling brown hair over it.

Aurora dropped a curtsy and found her hand caught in the man's damp warm fist, as he raised her back to an upright position.

"*Enchanté!*" the man said with a slight lisp.

He smiled at her, wiping a large white handkerchief over his round face and heavy jowls which were shiny with sweat from standing so close to the fire.

"That's French for '*pleased to meet you*'," he went on and laughed loudly again, ending on the same breathless squeak.

Aurora took a step back and retrieved her hand.

This strange person was behaving most oddly and she wondered if he might be a London acquaintance of her stepmother come to join them for the evening.

He looked to be of an age with Lady Hartnell.

"I thought that you might appreciate my use of the French phrase," he lisped, pursing his red lips into a bow, "as you are fresh from school in Paris, so they tell me."

Aurora looked round helplessly at her Papa.

Thank goodness Lord Moreton had not arriv as she would hate his first sight of her to be in con with this shiny-faced middle-aged creature.

Papa was smiling encouragingly at her, raising his white brows in a meaningful way and the large man was showing no signs of moving away from her.

His little beady eyes were fixed on Aurora in a very unpleasant manner as if he was trying to memorise every small detail of her face.

"There's no need to be coy, Aurora," came in Lady Hartnell from her perch on the sofa, "you knew that *Lord Moreton* would be joining us for dinner."

Aurora felt her mouth drop open with shock.

She had to struggle to stop herself from gaping like a goldfish as she was standing there, rooted to the spot on the drawing room carpet.

"Have you nothing to say for yourself?" added her father. "We don't usually find you at a loss for words."

Aurora was saved from having to make a reply by the entry of Treginnis, who loudly announced dinner.

She found herself on the arm of Lord Moreton, her hand placed on the slippery blue velvet of his coat, as the four of them made their way into the green-and-white glory of the dining room.

"Well," intoned Lord Moreton, "no expense spared here – that's what I like to see."

Aurora noticed how he lisped again and she quickly detached herself from his arm and sat down at her place.

"Yet another instance of your amazing good taste, Lady Hartnell," Lord Moreton rambled on, surveying the gleaming table. "Charming, perfectly charming!"

Aurora felt relieved that he did not appear to have seen that she had been in a rush to move away from him.

Now he was smiling and looking at Lady Hartnell in a somewhat familiar way.

Aurora wondered if her father had noticed this, but he was fussing over his chair and asking Treginnis to bring him another cushion for his back.

"Are you all right, Papa?" she asked softly, noticing that he was looking rather grey in the face.

"Naturally, my dear," he answered her quickly, "you are neglecting our guest! Where are your manners?"

Aurora took a deep breath and then applied herself to making polite conversation with Lord Moreton, which was very difficult, as he seemed to have little to talk to her about and she did not feel it was polite to keep introducing new subjects for discussion.

What became clear was that Lord Moreton liked his food, as he consumed a great deal of every course and then passed comments on everything he had eaten.

"Capital venison!" he declared, chewing heartily. "And does this come from your estate, Lord Hartnell?"

Lord Hartnell nodded.

"I must acquire some deer for the Park at Elton Hall as soon as may be," said Lord Moreton, wiping his mouth after clearing his plate completely, and, once again, Aurora saw him catch Lady Hartnell's eye.

Aurora could not touch her food and was reduced to moving it around her plate so that no one would notice, but this did not escape Lord Moreton's attention.

"Your daughter has a poor appetite," he remarked, watching her toying with a small helping of dessert. "We must put that to rights as soon as maybe!"

"And so what would you have in mind?" enquired Lady Hartnell, looking around for Treginnis to serve her a second helping of trifle.

"Aha!" Lord Moreton replied with one of his little breathless squeaks, "I expect she is missing the fine French *cuisine* she got used to on the continent. I'd like to wager she wouldn't turn her nose up at a dinner from my chef. He's French! I have nothing but the best at Elton Hall."

"We should just love to sample his *cuisine*," cooed Lady Hartnell smiling at Lord Moreton.

"Then we shall arrange it soon," he smiled back at her.

"And now, my dear, I think it is that time we ladies retired and left the gentlemen to their port and cigars," said Lady Hartnell as dinner drew to a close.

Aurora followed her into the drawing room feeling uneasy, as her stepmother seemed in such cheerful spirits and she could not understand why.

Lady Hartnell was smiling away to herself and half breaking into laughter.

Aurora was glad to find her sewing basket and took out her embroidery to wile away the time till the gentlemen came to join them.

But when the time came it was Lord Moreton alone who came to the drawing room, his shiny face flushed red from the port and his handkerchief flapping in his hand.

Swiftly Lady Hartnell rose from her chair.

"I must go to my husband," she said, giving Lord Moreton a sideways look, "and make sure that he has all he needs. He has been most out of sorts over Christmas."

With that Lady Hartnell left the room in a swirl of red skirts and Aurora was left alone with Lord Moreton.

She had been longing for and dreaming about this moment since Christmas Eve, but now it had come, she did not know where to look.

She only wished that she could be somewhere else – a long way from the drawing room of Hadleigh Hall.

The portly Lord Moreton then approached her and

staggered clumsily down onto one knee, as he pulled a long slim velvet case from the pocket of his blue coat.

"This may seem surprising, unforeseen, hasty even – " he began, and Aurora wished he did not lisp so badly or at least would choose words without so many s's in them.

He seemed be struggling to express himself as he wiped his face with his handkerchief before continuing,

"Our short acquaintance, however, has proved no hindrance in the increase of my affection, which already, from my conversations with your dear mother and father, had begun to blossom – "

'Oh, let him just propose,' thought Aurora, 'and I can say 'no' right away!'

He held out the velvet case and opened it.

Inside was an emerald necklace, a perfect match for the earrings that Papa had given her for Christmas.

"Here is a small token of my esteem – my deepest regard for your lovely self."

Aurora's heart turned over.

The necklace was very beautiful and she knew that it would look just perfect if she was to wear it. How had he known that it would be so right for her?

And then to her horror, she heard the words,

" – ask you to be my wife!" coming in a rush from Lord Moreton's mouth, as he dangled the necklace in front of her.

What should she do?

She must say 'no', of course, she could not marry this man.

And yet he did look rather pathetic, kneeling on the carpet in front of her, holding out the beautiful necklace of shining green emeralds.

Suddenly she realised that her own dear Papa must have helped him choose the necklace and that was why he had been so pleased that she had liked his Christmas gift of the matching earrings.

The situation was indeed a difficult one.

Lord Moreton seemed sincere as he was stumbling over his words in his nervousness and the lovely necklace had clearly cost him a great deal of money.

And Papa had told her so many times that he was in favour of the match and would be very proud of her if she became Lady Moreton.

'I must be careful,' she told herself, 'and I must not upset this man – that would be rude and impolite.'

"This has been very sudden," she said slowly, "and I must have some time to think."

"But – surely," he stammered, "you cannot hesitate. I am the – closest friend of your dear Mama and Papa. Our estates run side by side! And I am a wealthy man – you shall have every luxury you desire."

"Yes – " murmured Aurora.

"Ah! *Yes*, then, is your answer, as I knew it should be!"

Lord Moreton was now struggling onto his feet, a smile widening on his round face.

"No!" countered Aurora. "I was only agreeing with what you said just then, not agreeing to marry you! I must have some time to think."

Lord Moreton wiped his brow again.

"*Every luxury*," he repeated. "A French chef, all the dresses you could possibly wear – "

"You are very kind," she said again. "But you must allow me a little time – "

"To get used to the idea. Of course. But please, as a token of my esteem –"

And then he thrust the emerald necklace at her.

"No, no! I couldn't possibly!" she cried, trying to give it back to him.

"Do me the honour, Aurora, I beg of you! Then at least I may know that you have some affection for me and that you consider my proposal with respect."

"Of course I respect your proposal, but I cannot take something so valuable," persisted Aurora and tried again to hand back the necklace.

"It belongs to *you*," he exclaimed. "Your father and I chose it together. You must accept it!"

He was becoming quite agitated and Aurora longed for him to leave her alone in the drawing room so that she could try and puzzle out what she should do next.

"Just how can you not understand the depth of my feeling for you?" Lord Moreton continued, "how can you so insult me as to refuse this gift? You seem so heartless, and yet your father said you are a kind and thoughtful girl."

"I don't want to upset you," replied Aurora quickly. "If it means so much to you, Lord Moreton, of course I will keep the necklace. But I must ask you to leave me now to give me time to think over what you have said."

To her great relief, Lord Moreton wiped his brow again and made for the door, where he bowed and assured her that he would wait for her answer to his proposal with great anticipation.

She collapsed on the sofa clutching the necklace.

What had she done?

At least she had not agreed to marry the man.

And surely as soon as she had spoken to Papa, he would understand how she felt –

He was probably even now thinking after all he had seen of Lord Moreton at dinner that the whole engagement idea was a mistake.

It was too late now to disturb her Papa, who would probably be settled for the night, and she decided that the whole business could wait until the next day.

As she tiptoed upstairs to her room clutching the emerald necklace, she heard voices from a dark corner of the hall below.

Lady Hartnell was speaking,

"You should have tied it all up tonight, *you fool*!"

"I tried, Charlotte. She wouldn't play."

Was that Lord Moreton's voice?

Aurora leaned over the banister so that she could hear more clearly.

"We don't have all the time in the world, Robert! We cannot afford to delay or we will lose our little game!"

Lady Hartnell's whisper carried on up the stairs and Aurora shivered at the sound of it.

"Well, don't fret too much. She took the necklace, and so the deal is almost done," muttered Lord Moreton in a husky lisping whisper.

There was the sound of a door opening and closing and the voices faded away.

'*Charlotte*!' pondered Aurora, 'Lord Moreton is on first name terms with my stepmother, I am sure that cannot be proper.

'And what does he mean *the deal is almost done*? If he really thinks that I am going to marry him, he is very much mistaken.'

As she climbed up the last of the stairs and made her way to her room, her mind was turning over and over the words she had just heard.

CHAPTER THREE

The next morning as soon as it was light, Aurora made her way to the stable yard.

She had to get away from Hadleigh Hall for a few hours just to collect her thoughts and try to understand the feelings that kept welling up inside her.

Thomas, the young coachman, was sweeping up in the yard and as soon as he saw her, he straightened up and touched his cap.

"Good mornin', Miss Aurora," he grinned. "You'll be wantin' Aleppo, I expects."

Aleppo had always been her dear Mama's favourite horse, a beautiful grey Arab brought back by her Papa from his travels in Eygpt.

He was an old stallion with his frosty grey coat now turned white, but his eyes were still bright and there was a definite spring in his step – and Aurora loved to ride him.

Thomas went off to saddle and bridle Aleppo and then led him out so that he could help Aurora mount.

"You'll be wantin' me to accompany you, miss?" he asked, as it was usually his duty to follow along behind at a discreet distance when the ladies of the family went for a ride.

"No, Thomas, thank you, not today. I am going to visit Mr. and Mrs. Westcott at Valley Farm. There will be no need for you to come with me, I shall be quite safe."

Aleppo cantered gaily along the green track that led to the farm and Aurora felt suddenly close to her mother, who had spent many happy times exploring the countryside on the back of the same plucky little stallion.

'Oh, Mama,' whispered Aurora, 'what shall I do? I should feel that I am very lucky that someone so important and wealthy wants to marry me and that I should be happy and grateful – but it just doesn't feel right.'

Of course her Mama could not reply, but suddenly Aurora felt her spirits lighten as if someone had given her a hug and Aleppo tossed his head and leapt in the air with a joyful frolic.

Aurora's hat flew off, leaving her long auburn hair to fly free in the wind as they raced along and her troubled thoughts were swept away like so many cobwebs.

The Westcott's farm was a rambling cluster of old stone buildings nestling into the side of a steep green hill.

And as Aleppo's hooves clattered on the cobbles of the farmyard, two black-and-white sheepdogs ran up to her barking and wagging their tails.

Mrs. Westcott, a motherly woman in a blue apron, came out from the Farmhouse with her arms open.

"Why, it's Miss Aurora!" she exclaimed, her round face blushing red. "I thought that the clock had gone back twenty years. You are the very image of your dear mother! I thought it was her come back to bless us with her sweet presence."

Aurora felt tears springing into her eyes as she slid down from the saddle and let Mrs. Westcott embrace her.

"Not that I should be treating you like a child any more, Miss Aurora!" cooed the farmer's wife, wiping away her own tear.

"Now that you are so grown-up. Come away inside and you shall have a fine cup of tea."

Aurora led Aleppo across the yard and tied him up

in the stable, which was filled with the warm smell of clean hay and made her way back to the Farmhouse.

"How are you, Mrs. Westcott?" enquired Aurora, as she sat down at the scrubbed wooden table in the spotless farm kitchen with blue and white china on the big dresser, and copper pots and pans hanging on hooks above the fire.

"Well, I have not felt myself these last few months. Right down in the dumps I have been. I can't help thinking over the past and all the sad things that have happened.

"We still miss your poor mother, you know, even after all these years. And there's our dear little Ivy too, she often comes to mind. There's a sad feeling in this house, Miss Aurora, and sometimes I just can't shake it off."

Aurora recalled that several years before, when she was quite young herself, Mr. and Mrs. Westcott had lost a little daughter to a fever.

"I think it must be the hardest thing to lose a child, Mrs. Westcott," she said, taking the older woman's hand.

"Why yes, my dear, it is, and not a day passes but I don't think of her and sometimes I feel she is still here with me and it breaks my heart – "

Aurora suddenly felt a strange sadness come over her and looking up, she could see a small girl standing in the door that opened onto the narrow staircase that led up to the bedrooms.

All Mrs. Westcott's other children were grown-up, either married and gone away or working on the farm – so who could this little girl be?

She was about to ask Mrs. Westcott about the little girl, when the child looked at her with big grey eyes and then shook her head and ran away up the stairs.

"Mrs. Westcott, my hair has come down – may I just go upstairs for moment and make myself respectable?"

asked Aurora, feeling strongly that the little girl wanted her to follow her.

"Of course, my dear," agreed the farmer's wife. "I shall set the tea to brew."

Aurora hurried up the steps and sure enough there at the far end of the landing, the little girl was waiting for her.

Aurora's heart was beating very fast and she knew that something very important was happening.

Phyllis had spoken to her often about her mother's ability to 'see' things and how she felt so sure that one day Aurora would find the same power within herself.

"It's in your blood, Miss Aurora, just you wait and see," she had said, her dark eyes wide and serious as she nodded her head, looking just like a wise Cornish pisky.

"I think you must be Ivy, aren't you?" whispered Aurora and the little girl nodded her head slowly.

"And you feel sad that your Mama misses you so much, and that is why you have stayed with her."

The child backed away and put her hands over her eyes as if she was crying.

Aurora shivered and then remembered other times she had talked with Phyllis about her Mama and how she had believed in the power of Divine Love.

And how all the spirits that remained bound to the earth because of love or sadness or fear could be set free by that Love so they could take their rightful place in Heaven.

"Listen, Ivy, you have been very good to your dear mother, but now your work is done and it is safe for you to go. She will not miss you now – she will be happy for you that you have moved on to a better place – "

Aurora held out her hands to the child and felt love and tenderness flowing from her heart.

And then the deepest shock of joy poured through her body and as she looked up, the little girl was gone.

And a bright ray of winter sunshine was streaming through the window and shedding its light everywhere.

Aurora stood very still, feeling quite breathless and shocked as she realised that something extremely unusual had happened and that she had never experienced anything like it in her life.

She would have liked to stay there for a few more moments, just to put her thoughts together and try and stop her legs from trembling.

But footsteps were coming up the creaking wooden stairs and then a warm hand touched her on the shoulder.

Mrs. Westcott was standing behind her with tears in her eyes.

"*Why, I can't believe it*! Miss Aurora, I was sitting by the table and I heard you speak to someone up here and I was about to come and see if you were all right, because I know that there's no one except you upstairs and then I had the *strangest* feeling!"

"Please don't worry," answered Aurora, conscious that her hair was still tangled and that she must look very foolish standing at the top of the stairs.

"I am really fine – I just need to brush my hair – "

"I'm not worried, my dear," replied Mrs. Westcott, wiping her eyes and smiling. "I haven't felt this happy in a long time, it's as if all the sadness that's been hanging over this house has suddenly blown away like a big dark cloud and now the sun can shine again."

Aurora felt relieved.

Mrs. Westcott was very red in the face from crying, but she did look quite different from the woman who had been sitting down in the kitchen.

Her large blue eyes were shining brightly and the lines had vanished from her brow.

"Why, that is wonderful, Mrs. Westcott. I am sure there is nothing for you to feel sad about."

"But tell me, my dear, who was it you were talking to? I was very puzzled to hear you speaking like that when I knew there could be no one with you."

Aurora hesitated for a moment.

Should she tell Mrs. Westcott what she had seen?

She plucked up her courage.

"I saw a little girl. It was *her* I was talking to."

Mrs. Westcott's red face turned pale.

"What did she look like – this little girl?"

"She was very slim with big beautiful grey eyes," recounted Aurora, eyeing Mrs. Westcott anxiously in case she should be upset. "She ran up the stairs and then along the landing."

Mrs. Westcott took a deep breath and put her hands up to the sides of her face, holding her cheeks as she tried to contain her emotion.

"I knew it! That was our Ivy. You saw our Ivy!"

"I thought it must be her," said Aurora, taking Mrs. Westcott's hands and holding them tightly.

"Oh, my dearest Ivy! Did she speak to you? What did she say?"

"She didn't actually talk to me, Mrs. Westcott, but I think that she was trying to tell me that she loves you very much and that she has been staying here with you all this time, because she is worried about you being so sad."

"I have been sad, Miss Aurora, as you know. But I wouldn't want to keep my little girl here – "

Tears were welling up in her eyes again.

Aurora then squeezed Mrs. Westcott's hands as she explained what had happened on the landing – about how Ivy had vanished, leaving a feeling of utmost joy and the bright light of the sun streaming in through the window.

"Oh, Miss Aurora, what a really wonderful thing to happen. You have the skill your mother had. She spoke to me of it several times."

"What do you mean?" asked Aurora, remembering what Phyllis had told her about her mother. "Do you mean that my mother could see people who had passed on? Was that her skill?"

"It was much more than that, my dear. Why, a poor lost soul would come to her and she would help that soul find its way back to its proper home – in the Light!"

Aurora felt a shiver down her spine.

Phyllis had never spoken to her about anything like that, but all that Mrs. Westcott had just said did seem to describe very well what she had experienced at the top of the Farmhouse stairs.

"Thank you for telling me, Mrs. Westcott. I think that is what has just happened. Ivy has moved on now, she is happy and free and you can let go of your sadness."

Aurora felt much calmer now, her legs had stopped shaking and she felt strong and happy with the knowledge that what had just occurred was an experience her mother had also known.

"And now, I really must have to do something with my hair," she exclaimed, running her left hand through her auburn curls. "I look more than ever like a haystack!"

"Come along my dear in here," said Mrs. Westcott, laughing as she led Aurora along the landing, "this is Ivy's room – we've left everything just as it was. And there's a nice mirror on the washstand."

Ivy's room was small and cosy with a low ceiling, sloping down under the eaves with a small diamond-paned window looking out onto the yard below and Aurora felt so peaceful as she sat down on the stool in front of the mirror.

"Let me help you, Miss Aurora," suggested Mrs. Westcott, picking up a comb from the washstand.

Suddenly there was a clatter of hooves from down below and an uproar of dogs barking.

"Who can that be?" wondered Mrs. Westcott aloud. "It isn't time for the men to come back for their lunch."

She bustled over to the window and looked out.

"Oh, my goodness. Oh, dear me. Whatever next? Forgive me, Miss Aurora, I must go down right away."

And she then hurried out of the room and down the creaking stairs.

Aurora ran to the window and looked out.

Down below in the yard, she could see a tall man in a top hat on a spirited black horse, which was pawing away at the cobblestones and shaking its head as if impatient to be racing over the fields.

She heard Mrs. Westcott's voice and then saw her rushing up to the stranger and curtsying respectfully as she approached him.

The man raised his hat to Mrs. Westcott and Aurora saw that he had dark hair.

She leaned closer to the window and heard his deep voice faintly through the glass as he spoke to the farmer's wife.

The man seemed to be asking her for something.

Mrs. Westcott shook her head and pointed to the fields where the men were working.

She was looking flustered and as Aurora watched, she disappeared back into the house and then returned with the bell she used to summon the farm workers at mealtimes and rang it loudly.

'There must be an emergency, I will go down and see if I can help,' Aurora thought, and without further ado she ran the comb through her hair, twisted it into a quick knot and pinned it up at the back of her head.

She ran down the stairs and out into the farmyard, and the two sheepdogs stopped barking hysterically at the stranger and came to greet her with their tails wagging.

"No, Spot! No Ben!" she called quickly. "Be good boys now. Don't jump up."

She was so distracted in trying to calm the excited dogs that she had no chance to look up at the stranger on his horse, and she realised as she heard him speaking that she must appear very rude.

"And who might this be?" the man was saying, as his mount fidgeted and fought for its head.

'Why, he's speaking about me as if I were a farm girl,' thought Aurora gently attempting to restrain the over-affectionate dogs and pushing them away. 'That's not very polite of him at all!'

"One of your family, perhaps, Mrs. Westcott, that I have not been introduced to?" he queried.

Aurora looked up at him.

He was certainly a very striking looking man with a strong chiselled face.

As their eyes met, he swept off his top hat and then he stared down at her from his perch on the tall horse.

Aurora held his gaze proudly, but felt conscious of mud on the hem of her riding habit from her earlier gallop and that her hair was starting to slip from its pins.

"Why no, my Lord!" gasped Mrs. Westcott. "This is the young lady from Hadleigh Hall, only just returned from Paris. Lord Hartnell's daughter, Miss Aurora!"

The man laughed and bowed from the waist, as his impatient horse turned round in a circle, its hooves slipping on the cobblestones.

"Forgive me," he called down. "I have just come to the neighbourhood. I am therefore not in touch with what is happening on the Social scene."

There was something slightly mocking in his tone, and Aurora felt uncomfortable, but Mrs. Westcott took her hand and drew her forward.

"This is the Earl of Linford, Miss Aurora, our most distinguished neighbour."

Aurora was shocked at this revelation, as the Earl was rarely seen in the neighbourhood. Even her father had not spoken to the Earl for many years.

His ancestral Castle, although standing empty and in disrepair, was the most imposing building in the district.

The Earl was smiling down at her,

"So this is what they are teaching the young ladies in Paris these days, eh! How to cultivate a rustic style – mud on the skirts and a fresh country glow on the cheeks!"

Aurora found herself blushing under his mocking gaze and was glad of Mrs. Westcott's hand in hers.

And what right had this haughty Earl to comment on her appearance in that way?

At last he turned away from her and stooped to pat his black horse on the neck.

"My horse has cast a shoe," he announced, "and I don't want to risk laming him on these stony tracks. I have come to beg assistance from the good Mrs. Westcott and her husband."

"And all the men are away at the top of the farm seeing to the cattle, my Lord. I have rung the bell, but they are taking an age to come."

"You have a fine horse," came in Aurora who could not help admiring the fiery creature with its glossy coat and arched neck.

"Indeed I do, and I have high hopes for him on the racetrack this year, which is why I would not risk laming him," responded the Earl.

"Then we must send for the blacksmith, my Lord," suggested Aurora.

"But who should go?" queried Mrs. Westcott. "Oh, where is Mr. Westcott."

"He is coming now, look!" cried Aurora, as she saw two men running down the hill towards the farm.

It was Mr. Westcott and Adam, his youngest son.

The Earl then jumped off his horse and he and Mr. Westcott inspected the hoof with the missing shoe.

They both agreed that it was a proper job for the blacksmith, as Mr. Westcott was able to shoe a farm horse, but did not want to take the responsibility of shoeing such a valuable thoroughbred.

The Earl prepared to mount and ride down to the village, but Mr. Westcott stopped him.

"Do be careful, my Lord," he cautioned. "You risk bruising his foot on the rough road. Let's send now for the blacksmith. Adam, run to the village and fetch him."

Adam nodded and was about to set off, but the Earl looked impatient.

"How long will that take? Can he not ride to the village? I don't have all day to linger here, I am due back at Linford Castle shortly for an important meeting."

"I'm sorry, my Lord, but all our horses are working on the farm today and it will take even longer to fetch them and get them out of their harnesses," replied Mr. Westcott, shaking his head.

"There is always Aleppo," came in Aurora quickly. "He is very fast and Adam could ride him to the village."

Mr. Westcott looked very relieved and in a trice the grey horse was led out and Adam hoisted up onto his back.

"Your little stallion is a goodly beast too" remarked the Earl, as Aleppo sped off towards the village with Adam clinging on tightly.

"He was my Mama's horse. My father brought him back from Egypt."

"His breeding certainly shows," remarked the Earl, smiling at her.

Now that he was on foot and not looking down on her from a great height, he did not seem quite so daunting.

"I must thank you very much for your kindness in lending him," the Earl continued. "It is much appreciated."

Aurora assured him that it was nothing and that she was happy to help.

Now that he was so much closer to her, she found it hard to meet the gaze of his dark eyes.

"Miss Aurora is truly the kindest of angels," added Mrs. Westcott. "She always brings sunshine and happiness wherever she goes, just like her dear mother before her."

Much to Aurora's embarrassment, she went on,

"She has brought light back into our house today and all the sadness that has lain on us for so long has gone. It's a rare gift she has – and no mistake."

"Indeed so," said the Earl with a serious note in his deep voice.

He was no longer smiling and an introspective and thoughtful expression had come over his face.

Mr. Westcott led the thoroughbred to the shelter of the stables and Mrs. Westcott then invited the Earl into the Farmhouse to take some tea.

"Thank you, good Mrs. Westcott, but I should like to stay out here a while and breathe your fine fresh air and perhaps your charming neighbour will keep me company until the blacksmith arrives."

Aurora wanted to leave and head back to Hadleigh Hall, but of course without Aleppo she could not do so.

She would have to stay here for tea and make polite conversation with this unusual gentleman.

"It's so strange that we have never met before, my Lord," she commented after a moment's silence.

"Oh, but you have been in Paris," replied the Earl.

"Only for a year and before that I was at home at Hadleigh Hall for most of the time."

The Earl looked at her and she noticed that his eyes were no longer bright and sharp, but had become deep and wistful.

"Yes, I daresay. The truth is that I have spent very little time at Linford Castle. It is not a place where I feel at home."

"I should think it must be wonderful to have your own Castle to live in, my Lord."

The Earl smiled again.

"Mrs. Westcott is right! There is something bright and cheerful about you that is most appealing. May I make a suggestion to you, Miss Hartnell?"

He spoke gently to her without a trace of his former mocking tone and Aurora felt much more at ease, although she could not imagine what he was about to say to her.

"Linford Castle has a sad and cold atmosphere," he went on. "And I have finally decided that I must address this and do something to make my ancient family home a more pleasant place to be."

"I am sure that is a good idea," agreed Aurora, still puzzled as to where he was leading the conversation.

"I am meeting today with some expert restorers and repairers who are going to start work on the structure of the building. But I feel that something more is needed.

"The Castle needs a woman's touch, needs some of the brightness Mrs. Westcott spoke about earlier. I wonder, Miss Hartnell, if you would be prepared to come and visit the Castle to give me the benefit of your advice?"

The Earl looked directly into Aurora's eyes again, and she sensed a deep unhappiness coming from him and felt something stirring inside her – a desire to dispel that unhappiness and bring the glow back into his dark eyes.

"I should love to see your Castle, my Lord, I never have, even though it is not far from Hadleigh Hall and it will be an honour for me to visit."

"Then may I expect you this afternoon at tea time? If your fine little horse will not object to another outing?"

Aurora thought for a moment.

If she was at home in time for luncheon and then proposed taking a drive with Phyllis, surely her father and stepmother would have no objection to her going out that afternoon.

"Aleppo will need to rest this afternoon. He is too old to be cantering about all day."

A dark cloud then passed over the Earl's face and he turned away to gaze out over the rolling green hills that surrounded the farm.

"But," she continued, "I shall take the Governess cart and will be happy to drive by and call at the Castle."

The Earl laughed and turned back to her again.

"I shall be delighted to welcome you, young lady."

Aurora was then pleased to see that two horses and riders were speeding up the track from the village.

It was Aleppo and Adam escorting the blacksmith up to the farm.

Now she needed to hurry back to Hadleigh Hall and make herself presentable, so there could be no objection to her plans for the afternoon.

As the Earl cupped his hands to take her foot and swing her onto Aleppo's back, she realised something very strange.

She had not mentioned Lord Moreton's proposal of marriage to Mrs. Westcott and in fact she had not thought about him once during all these events of the morning.

Was this the right way for girl who was about to be engaged to behave?

CHAPTER FOUR

"Wherever have you been, miss" demanded Phyllis, as Aurora entered her room and rushed over to warm her hands at the blazing fire that was cheerfully filling the air with warmth.

"Just look at you, miss, with all that mud over your skirts. Whatever have you been doin'?" continued Phyllis, tugging at Aurora's habit with an exasperated expression on her pretty Cornish face.

"Don't worry, Phyllis, the mud will brush off when it's dry."

But Phyllis was still looking troubled, so she added,

"I have only been to see the Westcotts over at the farm."

"Why didn't you wait for me, Miss Aurora, and we could have gone together?"

"Oh, Phyllis, I am sorry. I know you love to take a ride with me. I just wanted to be alone this morning, I had so much to think about."

"That's what bothers me. You didn't speak a word last night when you came up after dinner, just 'thank you and goodnight' was all you had to say to me and then you go rushin' off this mornin' without so much as a goodbye."

"That was very rude of me, but there is nothing to worry about, honestly, dear Phyllis."

"I don't believe you, Miss Aurora," replied Phyllis. "Somethin' is up and you ain't a-tellin' me what it is. You always go quiet and then go off by yourself when you are worried about somethin'."

Aurora sighed, wondering how she could explain to Phyllis the extraordinary events of last night.

"And to really cap it all," continued Phyllis, "I was tidyin' up your dressin' table and I found this!"

And she held up the emerald necklace.

"Oh dear. I was hoping to keep that a secret."

Phyllis shook her head doubtfully,

"I don't know as that's such a very good idea, miss. Them are real emeralds as far as I can tell and this necklace must be worth a fortune. So what's it doin' then on your dressin' table?"

Aurora opened her mouth to speak, but the words just would not come out.

Phyllis carried on,

"And why, Miss Aurora, in the name of all that's good, have you not told me what happened with that Lord Moreton last night? You was all agog to see him and I was fully expectin' you to come back upstairs to me engaged to be married. And now you're not a-tellin' a word of what went on. *Why wouldn't I be worried?*"

Aurora allowed Phyllis to help her out of her soiled riding habit and then wrapping herself in a large shawl, she sat in her petticoats on a sofa by the fire.

"So," demanded Phyllis, "is there to be a weddin' or not? And if there is, what's to become of me? He's a wealthy man, I hears, and he'll have plenty of servants of his own at Elton Hall."

Aurora found her voice at last,

"Oh, Phyllis! Of course you will stay with me and be my maid, whatever may happen. I simply couldn't part with you – *ever!*"

She cleared her throat and then reached out to take the emerald necklace from Phyllis, reluctantly explaining that she had not yet agreed to marry Lord Moreton, but that she had asked him for time to think about his proposal.

"He did seem a bit upset, Phyllis," she added as she then held up the emeralds so that they caught the firelight in their deep green hearts.

"And he insisted that I should accept the necklace as a gift. I tried really hard to refuse, but I felt a bit sorry for him, and so in the end I agreed to take it. It's so very beautiful, isn't it?"

"Beautiful or not, Miss Aurora, why then ain't you tellin' me then about the man himself? Was he handsome? Was he young and lively? Will you be takin' him for a husband when you've had time to think it over?"

"Oh, goodness, Phyllis. I don't think so – he's as old as my stepmother and speaks with a lisp!"

Phyllis tutted and shook her head again.

"So why did you take the necklace from him then? It be as good as a promise to take an expensive gift like that from a man – "

Aurora jumped up and hugged her maid.

"Please, don't worry, dear Phyllis. I will tell Papa just how I feel and give him the necklace to return to Lord Moreton and all will be well."

But Phyllis sighed and was not at all comforted by Aurora's words.

"I knew you shouldn't have gone down to dinner wearin' them emerald earrings with a blue dress. *Blue and green should ne'er be seen*! No good will come of it, I feel sure."

"I tell you what," suggested Aurora quickly longing to bring a smile back to her maid's face. "Come with me

for a drive this afternoon. I have a special visit to make and
I know you will enjoy it too."

"What visit might that be, miss?"

"We are going to take tea – at a Castle!"

Phyllis brightened at the thought of it.

"But whoever has asked you?"

"It shall be a surprise. It is a friend of mine, who I
bumped into while I was at the Westcotts."

And so Phyllis had to be content, as it was time for
Aurora to dress for luncheon.

*

Only her stepmother was in the dining room.

"Will Papa be joining us?" asked Aurora hopefully.

"He is indisposed, Aurora, and he will be staying in
his room today and asks not to be disturbed," replied Lady
Hartnell.

Aurora's heart sank as she had been hoping that she
could speak to him about Lord Moreton.

"Much too much excitement has incapacitated him.
Parties every day are not advisable for an elderly man like
your father."

"Of course not. I do hope that he will recover very
soon."

"And you are quite the sly little minx, aren't you?"
added Lady Hartnell with a supercilious half smile on her
face.

"I just – don't know what you mean – " stammered
Aurora, shocked by her stepmother's unexpected comment.

"Oh, I think you do, Aurora. Your behaviour last
night was quite calculated and intentional, I am sure."

"No, really – "

Aurora could feel herself going bright red.

"It's a very clever ploy – to keep a man waiting. A tactic you must have picked up in France, I daresay. Lord Moreton is totally infatuated with you now you are playing with him like this."

Lady Hartnell was looking pleased with herself.

Aurora was about to speak up and explain that there were no tactics or ploys involved and that she was simply postponing the moment when she would give a firm '*no*' to Lord Moreton.

But she looked again at her stepmother and decided against it.

'I must speak to Papa,' she told herself, 'and get him on my side. I am sure he will understand exactly how I feel and will help me to explain everything.'

"And just how long do you intend to keep on toying with your suitor, you saucy little puss?" Lady Hartnell was asking.

"I have told him that I need time to think over his offer. That is all I have said to him and that is the truth."

Lady Hartnell laughed.

"There is no need to be coy with me, young lady! You and I both know what you are up to. You have the necklace and that in itself is a clear indication of where you are heading. You just want to make quite certain you have him properly at your feet before you give in. I take my hat off to you!"

Lady Hartnell rose from table and swept off to the sitting room, where she usually spent her afternoons lying on the sofa and playing patience.

Aurora's heart sank as she now realised that Lady Hartnell was fully expecting her to accept Lord Moreton's proposal and believed that her request for time was just a ruse to inflame his ardour.

There was nothing she could do without speaking to her father and Aurora decided to leave the matter until she had done so – and to make the most of her afternoon at Linford Castle.

*

Aurora always loved driving the Governess cart and her spirits rose as it rattled over the stony road, pulled by Cherry, her fat little pony from childhood days.

The cart was a trim little carriage, small enough to be easily driven by a young lady and yet not too small to accommodate both herself and her maid in comfort.

Phyllis clung onto the side of the cart and her nose, already red from the cold, peeped out of the big cloak she had wrapped round herself.

"So who is it then, this mysterious friend of yours?" she asked Aurora for the tenth time.

"You just won't believe me, if I tell you," laughed Aurora.

"I don't like surprises, as you well know, miss. I likes to know what I'm gettin' myself into."

"Oh, alright, Phyllis," muttered Aurora, taking pity on her. "We are going to take tea with an Earl!"

Phyllis gasped with disbelief and accused Aurora of teasing her.

"No, Phyllis, I am telling the truth. I was going to tell you about him, and lots of other things that happened while I was at the Westcott's farm, but you were so cross with me about the necklace that I didn't get a chance."

Aurora told her about the Earl's arrival at the farm, and how she had lent Aleppo to Adam so he could fetch the blacksmith to shoe the Earl's horse.

"I did him a service and so it is quite natural that he should invite me to go for tea."

The Governess cart swung round a bend in the road and, before them standing proudly on a green mound in the middle of a wooded valley, they could see the high stone walls of Linford Castle.

"What a magnificent building!" exclaimed Aurora, shaking the reins to make Cherry go faster, "but look, the windows are all broken – and it looks as if there is a tree growing out of the roof!"

"It's a sad lookin' place," agreed Phyllis, "though it seems like it was fine enough in its day."

They raced up towards Linford Castle and clattered over the bridge that led to the big wooden entrance gates.

There was a little door at the side of the gate and as they drove up, it opened and an old man in a leather apron stepped through and asked them what their business was.

"I have arrived here to take tea with Lord Linford," Aurora replied proudly and explained who she and Phyllis were.

The old man nodded and stepping back through the little door, he pulled the bolts on the big gates and slowly opened them so that the Governess cart could pass through.

Aurora caught her breath as she looked around the courtyard of Linford Castle.

Four high walls surrounded them with a tall tower in one corner and at one side by the gates a charming house had been built nestling against the wall.

But the courtyard looked much neglected.

The flagstones were all uneven and in some places elder trees had taken root and were growing up strongly, as if trying to claim Linford Castle back into woodland again.

The door of the house opened and the Earl stepped out, followed by two men in black carrying large rolled up pieces of paper.

"Welcome," he called out, his deep voice ringing around the courtyard. "I have been busy with my architect and my restorer, otherwise I should have come to the gates to receive you."

Aurora jumped down from the Governess cart and made a swift curtsy.

"Thank you, my Lord, for your kind invitation."

Phyllis was crouching down on the hard seat of the Governess cart, trying to avoid the Earl's eye, as she was completely overcome with shyness.

"And this is my maid, Phyllis."

Aurora reached for Phyllis's hand, encouraging her to step down.

"My Lord," muttered Phyllis respectfully, and then curtsied so low she was almost sitting on the ground.

"Your companion and amanuensis?" asked the Earl, "I am delighted you have brought her with you."

"My Lord," interrupted the taller of the two black-coated men, "to return to our discussion – "

The Earl raised his hand.

"This is Miss Hartnell," he said, "the daughter of Lord Hartnell of Hadleigh Hall. She will be included in our talks from now on, as I wish to know her opinion on the matters we are discussing."

The tall man looked put out.

"Is the young lady acquainted with the finer points of architecture?" he enquired with a sniff.

Aurora felt herself blush, as indeed she knew very little about architecture, but the Earl seemed not to have heard the tall man's comment and was inviting her to look at a plan that was being unfolded by the other black-coated man.

"Mr. Hodge, the architect, is in favour of razing my Castle to the ground and start afresh to build a completely new house," the Earl explained, glancing at the tall man who had spoken so rudely.

"But Mr. Nicholls over here is a restorer and if you look at his drawing, you will see that he prefers to keep the structure, repair it and build around what is already here."

Aurora felt her heart beat fast as she bent over the paper held by the restorer.

It was just so exciting to be consulted about such an important matter, even though the pencilled lines on it did not make very much sense to her.

"Which view do you take, my Lord," she asked the Earl after a few moments. "Would you see Linford Castle destroyed completely and the work begun again – or would you prefer to keep what is here? After all, it is you who will be living here."

The Earl laughed.

"I'm very glad I asked you to come. I knew you would go straight to the heart of the matter. Of course, the architect believes that he is right and so does the restorer. But I, who indeed will live here, simply do not know what I should do."

He turned to the two men.

"Thank you, gentlemen, for your valuable advice. I am going to take a turn around the Castle with this young lady and reflect upon my choices."

The architect and the restorer stepped back with a polite bow, although they both looked somewhat miffed.

The Earl smiled at Aurora and invited her to follow him as he strolled around the courtyard.

Aurora felt a shiver run through her as they walked towards the tower in the corner.

It looked very dark and forbidding with its smashed windows and endless trails of water running down its walls from broken gutters.

"This is a very sad place," she murmured.

"I think so too. There is nothing here that makes me really want to stay and when I see this tower, I think that perhaps the best option might be to knock the whole thing down – "

Aurora was about to agree with him, but something stopped her, almost as if someone had placed a finger on her lips.

"Let's move on," she suggested.

The Earl led her back to the courtyard with its four tall walls and explained that this was the oldest part of the Castle built many centuries ago by his ancestors.

"It is very quiet here," remarked Aurora, looking up at the sky framed by the walls. "We are in the middle of a beautiful wood, but there are no birds to be seen."

"They don't come," admitted the Earl, "ever since I was a child I have never seen a bird within these walls."

Again Aurora felt a shiver run through her body.

The place seemed so neglected and felt so dark and dreary that she longed to leave – to jump into the cart and drive swiftly away.

But again something held her back like a soft hand touching her arm.

"Is there anything here that you like?" she asked the Earl, "anywhere you can feel happy when you are visiting your Castle?"

"Let me show you something," he suggested and led the way to the house that was built into the Castle wall.

"This house was built by my grandfather," the Earl explained, as he opened the front door into the hall.

"It is lovely!" cried Aurora as she looked around.

In front of her across the marble floor, a gracious staircase swept up in a wide flowing curve, and all around the large hall were white painted doors she longed to open.

As if he had read her mind, the Earl walked over and gently pushed one of the doors open, revealing a tall room with pale green walls and ornate plaster decorations of cherubs and flowers on the walls and the fireplace.

Aurora caught her breath at the beauty of it all and then noticed that the furniture was covered in white sheets, so the room seemed to be inhabited by a crowd of ghosts.

She turned to the Earl,

"Why is everything hidden away like this?"

The Earl sighed.

"No one has lived here for many years since before I was born in fact. The sheets are to keep the dust away."

Aurora felt a wave of sadness pass over her as she looked up at the plasterwork above her head and saw that there was a coating of dust over the cherubs and the bunch of grapes that hung there.

"But come with me," said the Earl, again seeming to sympathise with her mood. "There is one place here that I particularly love."

They walked to the back of the house where there was an old door made of dark knotted wood.

The Earl drew an ancient iron key from his pocket and twisted it in the lock.

Aurora stepped in front of him through the narrow doorway and found herself bathed in light.

She was standing in a small Chapel with stained-glass windows of all colours and as the sun shone through the coloured glass, it made pools of green, red, yellow and blue over the stone floor.

She could not say a word, but drank in the beauty of everything around her.

She took in the intricate carved leaves and branches of the rood screen in front of her and beyond it the small altar with its golden crucifix.

At last she felt able to speak.

"There is no sadness here in this Chapel, my Lord, all I feel is joy and peace."

"It is the same for me. This is the one place where I feel truly peaceful and happy and for that reason, I still come back to the Castle. If it was not for this Chapel, I think I would have stayed away forever."

"But why does the Castle hold such unhappiness?" enquired Aurora.

"Perhaps I should share with you the tragic story of what happened here – if you would be prepared to listen?"

"Of course," agreed Aurora enthusiastically and sat down on one of the carved pews.

"My grandfather built this house inside the remains of our ancestral Castle many years ago when he was still a young man and he loved it dearly. He chose to live here most of the time, although he had many other fine houses and his two sons were born here."

The Earl paused for a moment.

"Oh, do go on, my Lord. I love to think of your family living here and growing up in this beautiful place."

"My uncle Charles was the elder and my father was the second son. They were the greatest of friends and my father was an adventurous young man who longed to travel the world as an Army Officer, so he bore no resentment that his brother Charles would inherit the family estate."

Again the Earl paused and Aurora knew that what he was about to tell her was causing him great pain.

"Both brothers adored the countryside and enjoyed the pursuits of a country gentleman.

"One day Charles and my father were cleaning their guns in the gunroom, which used to be in the old tower. My father did not realise that his gun was still loaded and as he picked it up, it went off and the bullet hit Charles and killed him!"

"Oh!" cried Aurora, feeling the shock and pain of that terrible event hit her like a blow. "How terrible! Your poor father."

"Yes," the Earl murmured, his face now dark with sadness. "Not only had he lost his dear friend and brother by his own hand, but he was now the heir to the estate and he must stay here in England, never able to forget what had happened."

"But it was an accident?"

"Indeed. And those who witnessed what happened absolved my father from any guilt. But he never recovered from that terrible day. And that, I do believe, is why this Castle is so full of grief and sadness and why no one has been able to live here ever since."

He turned to Aurora and took her hand, and she felt a wave of sensation pass through her as she felt his warm touch.

She closed her eyes for a moment and listened as he carried on speaking,

"After you left the farm this morning, I talked with Mrs. Westcott and she told me what had happened during your visit. She told me that you had brought sunshine and happiness back into her home and that you had done this by freeing the spirit of her long-dead daughter Ivy from her earthbound state – "

Aurora opened her eyes and found she was looking directly into the Earl's dark gaze.

"Yes – I think that's what – happened."

"And as soon as I heard her say that," continued the Earl, looking intently at Aurora, "I knew that I needed you here. The terrible sadness that hangs over the Castle, surely it must be because of the awful tragedy that happened to my father and his brother."

"It could be true," said Aurora, full of heartache as she thought of the pain the Earl's father had gone through.

"It could be that the spirit of your Uncle Charles has not been able to leave this place, or perhaps even your father has come back to try and make some reparation for what happened – "

She shuddered as she spoke.

She longed to move away from the Earl and from the unearthly darkness that she felt was beginning to gather around them.

The sun seemed to have gone in and the bright light that had been streaming through the stained-glass windows had faded.

"But can't you tell?" the Earl quizzed her urgently. "I was sure you would know what to do – that you would be able to help me."

Aurora took a deep breath.

"What occurred at the Westcott's Farmhouse had never happened to me before. It was the *first* time."

"But Mrs. Westcott told me that you had inherited a special gift – from your mother."

Aurora thought she would faint under the pressure of the Earl's passionate pleas.

"Yes, I really do believe that is the case, but you must understand, it was very different at the farm. Ivy was just a little girl. She appeared to me and when I saw her, I knew exactly what I needed to do.

"But here, this terrible tragedy that occurred within your family – I don't know how to help you."

The Earl's face fell and he looked despondent.

"I am so sorry," Aurora continued, as tears welled up in her eyes. "What you have told me today is so sad – I think it may be too much for me."

"It is I who should be sorry, Miss Hartnell. How could I have expected someone so young and gentle and sweet-natured to involve herself with all the darkness and tragedy that has manifested itself here?"

He took Aurora's other hand and she felt steadied and comforted, although her head was still spinning.

"Let me offer you some refreshment," the Earl was saying. "My coachman has made a fire and I will ask him to boil a kettle and make some tea for us."

They made their way back to the courtyard, where a few tiny snowflakes were beginning to drift down through the cold air.

"I wonder if I should head back to Hadleigh Hall right away," she murmured, looking up at the dark clouds that were massing in the sky.

"Alas, I keep no carriage here, as I live mostly in London and do not visit the Castle very often or I would have offered to have my coachman drive you back. You will be very cold in that open Governess cart."

"You are too kind, my Lord, but we will make good speed with Cherry between the shafts and I don't think we should linger any longer."

The Earl took her hand again and held it to his lips for a moment.

Aurora felt her heart beating fast as a new wave of sensation swept over her.

She felt happy and sad and vulnerable – all at once.

She did not know whether she wanted to stay at the Castle or escape as quickly as she possibly could and flee back to Hadleigh Hall.

Over by the tower a fire was burning and Phyllis was there warming her hands.

She was talking to Duncan, the Earl's coachman, who was a broad-shouldered handsome young man with a fine head of curly red hair.

When she saw Aurora, she came hurrying over.

"We should be on our way, miss, before this starts to settle," she insisted.

The Earl carefully helped Aurora into her seat in the Governess cart and handed her the reins whilst Phyllis clambered up after her.

"Goodbye, Miss Hartnell," he sighed, "I am most honoured by your visit this afternoon and I hope that it will not be too long before we meet again."

He bowed as the Governess cart swung out of the wide gates.

"Oh, Phyllis," exclaimed Aurora as they drove over the bridge, "I have so much to tell you, I don't know where to begin!"

"I daresay, Miss Aurora," replied Phyllis. "But first of all I needs to ask you somethin'."

"What is that?"

"What is an *amanuensis*?"

Aurora burst out laughing.

"I have no idea, but I will be sure and ask Papa to consult the dictionary, as soon as I get to speak to him."

"Thank you, miss, but I am a-wonderin' if we will ever make it home through this blizzard!"

Aurora's heart sank as she watched the snowflakes

that were now falling so thick and fast they were beginning to cover the road ahead.

"Don't worry Phyllis, we will soon be home."

But her words sounded hollow in her ears and she wished she could turn back to the safety of Linford Castle.

CHAPTER FIVE

The road climbed up out of the valley and Cherry puffed and panted as she pulled the Governess cart up the steep incline, forging ahead through the snowstorm.

"I hope we are going to make it," muttered Aurora, anxiously peering through the curtain of thick snowflakes.

"Just give the pony her head, Miss Aurora, she will find her way home," suggested Phyllis, her voice sounding faint and muffled through the thick scarf she was wearing.

The snow was falling so fast that Cherry was soon wearing a thick white blanket on her back and head, and as she plodded on it became harder and harder to see where the road was leading them.

Aurora could feel the weight of the snow settling on top of her hood and the cold and damp beginning to seep through the thick material of her cloak.

She began to fear that they would have to spend the night outside on the road and would never make it back to Hadleigh Hall.

"What is that!" cried Phyllis suddenly, clutching at Aurora's arm.

There was a crunching sound of footsteps trampling through the snow and over her shoulder Aurora could see a blurred shape drawing near through the blizzard.

"I don't know, Phyllis," she mumbled, her heart in her mouth. "It could be anything. I can't quite see."

"Hallo!" a faint cry came to them. "Bear left, keep to the left or you will come off the road!"

The dark shape loomed nearer and Aurora realised that it was a horse and rider, leaping and plunging over the hillside to join them.

"*It's the Earl*, Phyllis! I would recognise his big black horse anywhere!"

The Earl then came along the side of the Governess cart and swept off his hat, allowing the snowflakes to settle on his dark hair.

"My apologies if I startled you, Miss Hartnell, but I could not let you make this journey alone. I know the road well and I hope you will allow me to accompany you."

"Thank you very much, my Lord, I was beginning to fear that we would lose our way."

"I will ensure you reach home safely," persisted the Earl. "Guide your pony to follow in my tracks."

And he urged his black horse forward to lead the way through the blizzard.

The journey seemed to last forever and Aurora was so grateful for her gallant escort, as she resolutely followed his shadowy outline through the swirling snow.

At long last the brick pillars of the lodge gates of Hadleigh Hall appeared through the snow and she called out her thanks to the Earl.

"It is nothing at all, Miss Hartnell," the Earl replied, brushing the snow from his coat collar and smiling at her.

"We will be quite safe now, Cherry knows the drive up to the Hall as well as she knows her own stable and we have no further need of your kind help, so farewell."

"But you *must* permit me to escort you safely to your door."

"No, please," answered Aurora quickly. "There is no need."

She was filled with horror at the thought of trying to explain the Earl's presence to her stepmother.

The Earl edged his prancing horse up closer to the Governess cart and looked into Aurora's face.

"I am most reluctant to say goodbye to you, Miss Hartnell. I feel I have burdened you with too much of my own troubles and sadness today."

"Not at all, my Lord. You have been very kind to accompany us all this way through such a bad snowstorm."

"It was a pleasure, I assure you," smiled the Earl, "but I would like to ask something more of you."

Aurora suddenly felt warm all through despite her cold wet cloak and frozen ears and fingers.

"I would appreciate a little more of your company, but this time in much more congenial circumstances. Will you dine with me tomorrow night?"

His dark eyes were shining and his smile flashed at her through the drifting white flakes.

Aurora was about to agree to his invitation when she suddenly remembered that she was just a young girl – and a young girl who was as good as engaged.

Her father and her stepmother would never permit such a rendezvous.

"I am sorry, my Lord, but I don't think I can. My father and stepmother would not allow me to accept."

"Of course, Miss Hartnell. Please forgive me, you seemed such an intrepid and independent young lady when you drove through the gates of Linford Castle."

Aurora realised that she should shake the reins and urge Cherry to trot away home up the drive, but she could not bring herself to do it.

She could see that the Earl was still smiling at her, his eyes bright with expectation.

"I have an idea!" he said. "I would not wish in any way to compromise your reputation. But what if – "

He hesitated, looking mischievously at Aurora and Phyllis.

"Go on," urged Aurora hesitantly, for she knew that she should now bid him farewell and yet she did so want to know what he was about to say to her.

"There is a fine old inn down by the river where the food is excellent. What if we were to dress ourselves as local folk – perhaps a well-to-do carter and his wife – and visit incognito for our dinner?"

Aurora gasped.

She did not know what to say.

The plan sounded like so much fun and she would love to talk more to the Earl and to see him in a happier mood even though she knew full well it was not possible.

The Earl was continuing, undeterred by her silence,

"Your fierce lady's maid will act as chaperone and she will be able to help you with your disguise."

Phyllis was so shocked that her hood fell back and she stared at the Earl with her mouth open.

Aurora's head was spinning.

She felt that she had never been in such a difficult position before, since she was longing to accept the Earl's invitation and yet was quite certain that if she did so, she would cause distress to her father and make her stepmother very angry indeed.

'If only Mama was waiting at home for me,' she thought, 'and I could ask her what I should do.'

The chilly wind then lessened and Aurora blinked

the snowflakes from her lashes and looked around her to see Hadleigh Park transformed into a white wonderland.

All at once she knew what she could now say that would neither hurt his feelings nor compromise herself,

"Thank you, my Lord, for your kind invitation. I'm sure it is a most entertaining idea. But I do not think it will be possible for me to go out while the weather remains so unpleasant."

The Earl look around and then laughed.

"You are right, Miss Hartnell, forgive me for being so impatient. This snow may be on the ground for many days and it's surely not a good time to be gadding about."

He turned back to her and looked at her intently.

"But please, do promise me that as soon as the thaw comes and the sun is shining, we may have our meeting."

Aurora looked away in confusion.

This was the second time in twenty-four hours that a man had pressed her to make a promise and this time, unlike her experience with Lord Moreton, she wished that she could say '*yes*'.

The Earl seemed to appreciate that she was feeling confused and he did not insist that she reply immediately.

"I shall send for you," he called, as his black horse tossed its head, "as soon as the snow has melted."

Aurora watched his shadowy outline merge into the falling snow and her heart felt warm with joy.

She had not said anything she should not and had made no promise that she could not keep and yet she was sure that she would see the Earl again.

Phyllis plucked at her sleeve.

"Miss Aurora," she exploded hoarsely, "I am frozen to the bone. And I'm not sure I like being called 'fierce'!"

"Oh, Phyllis," Aurora replied, as she urged Cherry on. "I am sure the Earl did not mean anything nasty. He simply knows that you always take very good care of me."

"That's as may be," huffed Phyllis. "Askin' you to meet with him in secret – with all this snow on the ground. Your tracks would be as plain as pikestaff!"

Aurora was wondering what Phyllis meant.

If she was worried about their tracks being seen in the snow, was she actually thinking about the possibility of a secret meeting with the Earl?

But before she had time to ask her what was on her mind, the Governess cart reached the gravel circle in front of Hadleigh Hall and they were home at last.

*

The next morning after breakfast, Aurora took the emerald necklace, wrapped it up in a silk handkerchief and tucking the bundle into the waistband of her dress, knocked lightly at the door of her father's bedroom and heard his faint voice instructing her to enter.

The room was pleasantly warm from a huge fire in the grate and was filled with a wonderful clean white light reflected up from the snow on the lawns outside.

Her Papa, wearing a heavy silk dressing gown with a fur collar, seemed very pleased to see her and told her to sit comfortably by the fire as he rang the bell for the maid to bring her a cup of hot chocolate.

"I am so sorry, my dear and most lovely daughter, that I was indisposed yesterday morning, as I was of course hoping to speak to you about your talk with Lord Moreton. I am delighted that you were pleased with the necklace."

His obvious pleasure in her company and the fact that he was delighted she had accepted the necklace from Lord Moreton made it very difficult for Aurora to tell him her real feelings, but she knew that she had to do it and the sooner the better.

"Papa," she started, struggling to keep her voice from trembling. "The necklace is beautiful and I could not help but think that you must have helped Lord Moreton to choose it."

He laughed and his eyes twinkled with pleasure.

"How observant of you, Aurora. Yes, indeed, my good friend Lord Moreton asked me for my advice in the matter and I was most happy to assist him."

Her heart was sinking further with each minute that passed, but she had to continue,

"Papa, I should not have accepted the necklace – it was very wrong of me – "

"My dear," he interrupted. "In other circumstances perhaps it would not have been prudent to receive such a gift. But as you are going to marry this man – "

"I have not said so – yet," stammered Aurora. "I – have not replied – to his proposal."

"But you will, of course, my dear," said her father, the smile on his face looking a little less joyful.

"No, Papa, *no!*"

Aurora forced the words out.

"*I cannot!*"

She waited for her father to frown and to be angry with her, but he merely looked puzzled and a little sad.

"I just don't understand. This man, Lord Moreton, is a dear friend of both your stepmother and myself and is a perfect match for you."

Aurora felt a wave of despair pass over her.

How could her father not see that she did not like Lord Moreton?

That his looks and his lisping voice and everything he said were utterly repugnant to her.

How could he not have noticed this, when they had dined on Boxing Day?

Lord Hartnell continued,

"He is rich, he speaks French – at least a little – and he has a French chef. He lives close by, a circumstance which gives no little pleasure to me, as it means that I will then be able to see you almost every day and he loves you deeply and will look after your every need."

"I am so very sorry, Papa, but I cannot marry him," Aurora cried desperately. "I should never have taken the necklace and I beg you, Papa, please to take it from me and to give it back to him with my most sincere apologies."

She pulled the little bundle from her waistband and held it out to her father.

He took it from her most reluctantly, unfolded the silk handkerchief, pulled out the necklace and held it up to the window.

The vivid green fire that burned in the heart of the stones seemed especially beautiful in the clear white snow light that poured through the window.

Aurora felt so sad that such loveliness should be the cause of so much unhappiness.

"I simply cannot comprehend the reasons for your behaviour," he sighed wearily, "but I must trust that your feelings are sincere and you are telling me the truth when you say that you cannot marry this man."

He sighed again and looked even sadder.

"Just for a moment, then, when you were speaking, you took on the same look of your dear mother, who was the most honest and trustworthy of women."

Aurora longed to run and put her arms around him, but she did not know if it was the right moment.

And so she stayed where she was sitting in the chair by the fire, hoping with all her heart that her father would do as she asked.

He sighed even more deeply.

"To bring such bad news and such pain to a friend is something I will find most difficult, but it must be done and I will undertake to do it."

Aurora could hold back no longer and jumped up to hug him, but he did not respond to her affection and made no attempt to return her embrace.

"I am most disappointed in you, Aurora. And now I ask you to leave me alone. I must gather my energies for this most unpleasant task you have given me."

"Papa, I am so sorry, please believe me. And thank you, thank you so much – "

But Lord Hartnell was not listening and waved his hand to dismiss her.

There was nothing more that Aurora could say and she could feel tears welling up in her eyes, so she made a quick curtsy to her father and hurried out of the room.

As she ran down the stairs she saw that the servants were sweeping the hall and had left the front door open.

Holding back the sobs that were building up inside her, Aurora ran through the door.

She made her way across the dry powdery snow to the long terrace that looked out over the Park and stopped there for a moment, where no one could see her, to let her tears flow freely.

'If only Mama was here,' she thought, 'and I could ask her advice. What would she say to me? Surely she would understand how I feel.'

The sun came out suddenly through a small gap in the clouds and lit up all the little ice crystals that lay on top of the snow, so that the Park looked as if it was covered in tiny diamonds.

Aurora caught her breath with delight at the beauty of the scene in front of her and felt her tears drying on her face in the fresh breeze.

It was as if her Mama was standing right beside her, and showing her the richness and abundance of the world.

Aurora seemed to hear a voice whispering to her,

'Just look, my dear, there are other precious things in the world besides emeralds – '

'All will be well,' Aurora told herself and turned back to the Hall.

As she entered, she saw her stepmother standing at the bottom of the stairs, as if she was waiting for someone.

Aurora's heart skipped a beat as she saw that her face was like a thundercloud.

She realised that her stepmother must have been to her father's room and heard that the engagement was off.

Lady Hartnell did not say a word to Aurora.

She was simply glaring at her menacingly as if she was too contemptible even to speak to.

And then she turned aside to give an order to one of the footmen on duty.

Aurora slipped past the two of them, still expecting at any moment to be scolded, but her stepmother remained in icy silence.

It was with great relief that Aurora ran up the stairs and gained the safety of her bedroom.

As she stood by the fire to catch her breath, she saw a horseman in a big black cloak setting off down the drive, his horse's hoofs leaving deep prints in the soft snow.

'Who can that be?' she wondered. 'It looks like one

of the coachmen on an errand, but why is he going out on a day like this? The errand must be a very important one.'

She sat on a chair by the window and forgetting the unusual sight of the horse and rider setting off through the snow, found herself suddenly happier.

Her interview with her father had gone well and he had promised to return the necklace, so now Lord Moreton could not hold her to the engagement.

Her worries were over.

And so, as she picked up her embroidery, she found herself smiling at the delightful thought that now there was nothing to stop her seeing the Earl of Linford again.

*

The sun was falling lower in the sky and turning the expanse of snow in the Park to a rosy pink.

Phyllis brought in a tray of tea and toast and asked Aurora what she would like to wear for dinner.

"Why, Phyllis, I don't want to go down for dinner tonight at all. I should much rather stay quietly here in my room."

Phyllis frowned.

"I thinks they'll be expectin' a guest tonight, Miss Aurora, and they will be wantin' you to join them."

Aurora sighed.

The thought of having to sit through the meal under Lady Hartnell's cold stare was not a pleasant one, and she was not sure of how her father would be after the difficult conversation of a few hours earlier.

She glanced out of the window and there was just enough light still for her to see two horsemen approaching the Hall and her heart leaped with anticipation.

"Phyllis, look over here," she whispered. "Someone is coming. Do you think it could be the Earl?"

Phyllis peered out of the window.

"No indeed," she replied with a snort, "it's Thomas, the coachman and someone else who be short and fat and *most* unlike the Earl."

Aurora looked again and saw that Phyllis was right about Thomas.

She second person she could not recognise although she noticed that he was bouncing around in the saddle as his horse trotted through the snow and did not seem to be a very good rider.

"Maybe that is the guest, Phyllis, although I cannot think why he would wish to visit us on a day like this."

"It's curious, miss. Anyone with sense would stay by their own fireside with deep snow on the ground."

They looked at each other for a moment and then Aurora told Phyllis about her stepmother speaking to the footman earlier that day and the rider she had seen setting out on an errand.

Phyllis shook her head.

"Somethin's up, Miss Aurora!"

"I think so too."

She remembered the conversation she had overhead between her stepmother and Lord Moreton on Boxing Day.

Could it be that Lady Hartnell had sent Thomas to fetch him?

"Phyllis," she said quickly, "I am not feeling at all well. I have a bad headache and I shall stay in my room tonight, please tell my father and stepmother and apologise to them for me."

Phyllis nodded and hurried away.

Aurora drew the curtains and hid herself under the bedcovers, straining her ears to try and catch the sound of voices from downstairs.

All was quiet and still until after a while, she heard the sharp tapping sound of her stepmother's heels on the landing outside and the bedroom door abruptly opened.

"She is very poorly, my Lady," she heard Phyllis's voice whispering, "she should be left to rest quietly."

Aurora could then hear the rustle of Lady Hartnell's skirts as she approached the bed and smelt the heavy scent she always liked to wear in the evening.

She closed her eyes tightly turning her face to the pillow as she felt the bedcovers lifted from her shoulders.

"Why, you have gone to lie down with your clothes on!" came her stepmother's rasping voice. "You must be very ill indeed if you could not take the time to undress."

Aurora kept her eyes closed and tried not to blink, as she heard Phyllis say,

"Yes, my Lady, she is blind with her headache and had to lie down right away – look, see how pale she be."

Aurora held her breath, waiting for Lady Hartnell to shake her and pull her out of the bed and onto her feet, but nothing happened.

She felt the soft covers fall back over her shoulders again and then heard her stepmother's heels tapping as she walked away.

"Poor child," said Lady Hartnell her voice suddenly soft. "I shall send my maid with the remedy that I always take for the migraine. And, of course, she must not come down to dinner. I will inform Lord Hartnell."

She rustled over to the door still speaking,

"Our guest will no doubt be very disappointed, but what can we do? I shall leave the young lady in your very capable hands, Phyllis."

With that she was gone closing the door behind her.

Aurora opened one eye carefully to make sure that her stepmother had really left the room and then sat up.

"Well, I thought she would have dragged me from the bed, but she seems to believe that I am really ill."

"I don't know," remarked Phyllis. "She's a sly one for sure and it's hard to read what she's a-thinkin'."

"At least I am to be spared having to dine with Lord Moreton! For it is he who has just arrived, isn't it?"

"Yes, Miss Aurora. He be sittin' in front of the fire with your Papa."

She gave a deep sigh of relief, as she pictured Papa breaking the news to Lord Moreton and then returning the necklace to him.

"All is well, Phyllis!" she said, and explained what she had agreed with her father that morning.

Phyllis looked relieved to hear the news.

"Just as well then you're not goin' to be downstairs tonight. For I'm sure that gentleman will not be pleased with what your father has to tell him."

The boom of the gong announcing dinner sounded.

And now that she knew her stepmother and father together with Lord Moreton would be safely seated at the table, she slipped out of bed to sit on the sofa.

She and Phyllis sat beside the fire for a long time, talking through the events of the last few days until Phyllis confessed that she was feeling hungry.

"Oh, I am so sorry, Phyllis, you must go down right away. Cook and the others will be eating in the kitchen and I had quite forgotten that you should be with them."

"I don't like to leave you, Miss Aurora – "

"I shall be alright and perhaps you will be able to smuggle a little bread and cheese upstairs for me, since I have missed dinner."

Phyllis said that she would see what she could do and departed for the kitchen, leaving Aurora on the sofa.

She sat watching the fire die down, leaving dark red embers in the grate.

It was so peaceful in her room with just a couple of candles burning.

Sometime later she yawned, as she realised it must be getting late and time that she should be thinking about sleeping, although she was beginning to feel quite hungry.

She was just about to get up from the sofa and go to bed when she heard a faint noise on the landing outside.

"Phyllis?" she called out, "I hope that you got some bread and cheese for me."

There was no reply.

The candles had been burning for several hours and one of them guttered and went out.

Aurora stood up and went over to the door to meet Phyllis, her stomach rumbling loudly in anticipation of the food she brought.

She then opened the door onto the dark landing and a strong smell of port and cigars hit her nose.

"Phyllis?" she called out again, puzzled as to why her maid had been drinking and smoking.

Suddenly someone seized her arm in a harsh grip, bruising her soft flesh.

Aurora struggled to free herself and heard a thick lisping voice whispering in her ear,

"My Sweetheart!"

It was Lord Moreton.

CHAPTER SIX

"*No*!" Aurora cried, struggling to free herself from Lord Moreton's tight hold on her arm.

"Ah! Why do you hide yourself away like this?"

He slurred, his lisp more pronounced than ever and he lunged forward through the door, so that his face came close to hers as she caught the smell of wine on his breath.

"How could you cause me such unendurable pain?" he whinnied. "You are such teasing capricious creatures – you women! You know only too well that to deny us is to increase our ardour for you!"

Lord Moreton's grip on her wrist tightened sharply and Aurora bit her lip from the pain.

He seemed to be extremely short of breath and was puffing and panting as he loomed over her.

"My angel, you know that you are mine," he hissed, "mine for now and for ever."

He leaned forward as if about to kiss her, but then suddenly swayed backwards again.

'He must be extremely drunk,' Aurora decided, 'he can hardly stand up.'

She stopped trying to free her arm from his grip and leaned into him, as if she also was trying to snatch a kiss.

"My lovely one," he howled. "I knew that I should come to you and that then you would see sense."

The faint light of the candle in her bedroom showed

her that he was smiling broadly as he dropped her wrist and reached out with both arms to pull her body against his.

Aurora jumped backwards dodging out of his grasp, and as Lord Moreton swayed heavily in the doorway as he struggled to keep his balance, she seized a cushion from the sofa and hurled it at him.

"You little minx!" he yelled, falling back onto the door and catching hold of the cushion, as he gave one of his high-pitched squeaking laughs that so irritated her.

"Why, you fancy a little sparring match, do you?"

He tossed the cushion aside and then raised his fists and made a couple of boxing gestures.

"Come along then, come and let us see who shall prevail!"

He laughed again and took a distinctly wobbly step backwards towards the door, as if he was trying to build up momentum to take a run at her.

Aurora saw her chance and seizing the door handle, shoved the door against his portly stomach, pushing him back outside onto the landing.

"Faugh!" Lord Moreton exclaimed indignantly as the heavy door knocked the breath out of him.

Aurora leant against the wooden panels with all her strength, struggling to shut him out, but Lord Moreton still had one foot inside her bedroom, and he was a bulky heavy man while Aurora was a slim light girl.

She put her shoulder to the door and braced herself, pushing with all her might, but the door would not close.

Desperately she looked for a chair or anything that she could use to hold the door, but there was nothing at all within reach.

"*Open up!*" Lord Moreton shouted, "I will not be treated like this!"

The panel beneath Aurora's shoulder shuddered as he struck it with his fists.

She could not hold the door any longer and giving up the struggle, she ran across the room and took refuge behind the sofa.

But Lord Moreton, instead of pursuing her over the room, lost his balance completely as the door swung open, and then fell headlong through the door, like an immense avalanche in his velvet coat and onto the bedroom carpet.

He hit the floor with a crash and lay there wheezing and groaning, so that Aurora caught her breath anxiously, fearing he had hurt himself quite badly.

She watched him for a moment and he did not stir or make any attempt to rise up, so that Aurora was sorely tempted to skip past him and escape through the open door onto the landing.

But what if he really was injured?

He did not sound at all well and she feared to leave him in such a state, so cautiously she approached his heavy body where it lay sprawled on the floor.

She was almost there when suddenly his arm shot out and she felt her skirts caught and found herself being pulled forward.

Lord Moreton had recovered himself and had now seized hold of the hem of her dress.

"Look what have you done to me!" he cried with a pitiful wheeze.

"I am so sorry," said Aurora, trying to back away, "I did not mean for you to fall. I hope you are not hurt."

"I am mortally wounded," he moaned, as he heaved himself up onto his elbow. "You have stabbed me in the heart with your capricious behaviour."

Aurora tugged at her skirt, but she could not free it from his clutches.

"I apologise if I have misled you, Lord Moreton, but I cannot marry you."

"*Misled*!" he yelled. "You have destroyed me."

"I am so sorry, but I think it would be best if you left me now. I don't think it is right that you should visit me in my room."

"I have no intention of leaving you. Here I lie in my rightful place at your feet and I shall *not* budge until I have received the answer I desire."

He then moved his hand to get a firmer grasp of her skirts and she felt him trying to pull her down to his level on the bedroom carpet.

She resisted, tugging the fine silk of her dress away from his grasp and as he tugged back, she felt some of the stitches at her waistband give way.

Why had Phyllis been gone so long?

And whatever was she doing down in the kitchen?

Surely she had not been gossiping with the cook all this time. If only she would come back now and release her from this awful predicament.

"I must ask you to leave," she demanded. "I have spoken to my father and told him how I feel and he would be most upset if he knew that you had come to my room."

He laughed his high squeaking laugh and reached up to catch Aurora's wrist again, using his weight to drag her down so that she was kneeling on the floor beside him.

"You little fool," he burbled. "Do you really think that silly old man knows I am here?"

"Don't you dare speak of my father in that way!"

"Why on earth not? He's in his dotage and scarcely knows what is going on under his own roof."

Aurora felt tears springing into her eyes and a great rush of fear as she realised that she was on her own – there was no one who could help her escape the clutches of this most unpleasant man.

"He told me you had refused my proposal and gave me back the necklace, the purchase of which, I might say, gave me much trouble and much expense," continued Lord Moreton. "And then he retired to his room."

"Oh, poor Papa," cried Aurora. "He did not want to break the news to you, it must have upset him very much."

"That is as may be, but as soon as he had left me, I realised what I must do."

"No!" cried out Aurora, as he loosed her skirts and seized her other hand, pushing her backwards and down to the floor. "*Please.* I must ask you to leave."

"There is no one to hear you," he breathed hotly on her cheek. "You may squeal as much as you wish!"

"Stop this!" Aurora gasped, as she felt his weight crushing her against the carpet. "You are hurting me!"

"I am glad of that," Lord Moreton hissed, "for you have given *me* enough pain these last few days."

Aurora was now pinned firmly onto the floor by his bulk, but she could still move her head, so she could twist her face away in a desperate attempt to avoid the kisses he was forcing onto her lips.

"You may struggle," he gurgled, his mouth against her ear, "but I will *not* be denied. I will have you for my wife, whether you wish it or not!"

Aurora could scarcely breathe, trapped beneath him as she was and the feel of his moist lips against her skin made her shudder with horror.

Somehow she must try and free herself and alert the servants and her father to what was going on.

"Help!" she screamed. "I cannot breathe! You are stifling me!"

"I now have you where I want you – and I have no intention of letting you go!"

Lord Moreton tightened his grasp on her arms.

"*Help me!*" she shouted even more loudly.

"Phyllis! Anybody. Please I am in distress, I need your help!"

Surely somewhere out on the landing, there must at least be a parlour maid, tending to the fires or turning down the beds.

Lord Moreton clapped a hand over her mouth.

"I would not be so hasty in calling out for help," he lisped. "You are in a most compromising position, Miss Hartnell. Are you quite sure you would like your servants to see you locked in this intimate embrace with me?"

Aurora's heart turned to ice as she heard his words.

It might seem to anyone entering the room that she and Lord Moreton were clinched in a passionate embrace.

But now one hand was free and she had a chance of escape, which she must make the most of.

His heavy left hand smelling strongly of cigars was pressing down on her lips, and Aurora, feeling sick as she did so, seized the base of his thumb between her teeth and bit down on it as hard as she could.

Lord Moreton gave a shrill scream of pain.

Quick as a flash Aurora pulled her free hand from beneath him and caught him by the left ear, twisting it so that he screamed again.

In that same instant she used every last drop of her strength to push his heavy body off her, wriggling away as fast as she could and aiming to put the sofa between them.

But she was not quite fast enough and once again he had caught hold of her skirts – shouting with rage and pain he dragged her back towards him.

Aurora could not endure to be caught again and this time she fought back at him till the delicate stitching at her waistband gave way and the fine silk tore, leaving her in her petticoats and Lord Moreton clutching her torn skirts.

"You have bitten me like a wild animal, you little hussy!" he shouted, shaking his hand angrily. "Why, you have drawn blood, you vixen!"

Aurora clung steadfastly onto the back of the sofa, prepared to defend herself again, but before Lord Moreton could take another lunge at her she heard a welcome sound from the landing.

"Mind your language," she warned him, "for I hear footsteps."

Lord Moreton turned to glance at the door, sucking at his wounded thumb, and Aurora prayed that it would be Phyllis whose steps she had heard.

The footsteps halted just outside the door.

Aurora's heart sank as she caught a faint breath of the scent Lady Hartnell always wore.

It was her stepmother who was coming.

Aurora picked up one of the cushions and clutched it to her stomach, instinctively trying to hide the fact that she was only in her petticoats.

But, of course, she could not hide the fact that Lord Moreton was still holding her silk skirt.

There was a rustle from outside and the powerful sweet scent grew stronger as Lady Hartnell slowly entered the room.

She was carrying a tall candle that lit up her angular face and made her look even more forbidding than usual.

"Well, well, well," she muttered coldly, "and what has been going on here?"

Lord Moreton continued to suck his thumb and then stared at her like a sulky child.

"I could hear screaming and roaring fit to rival the zoological gardens just a moment ago," said Lady Hartnell, "and now neither of you can utter a squeak – "

She advanced further into the room and took up the piece of torn skirt from Lord Moreton, holding it up to the candle to inspect it.

"And clearly," she remarked with great disdain, "it is not just the noise you have been making that is worthy of the animal house."

"She bit me, the little whore!" cried Lord Moreton, and held out his hand to Lady Hartnell.

"Oh dear, my poor Robert!" Lady Hartnell laughed, "I told you she was ungovernable and wild. Why did you not take more care?"

Aurora felt a strong sense of unease, just as she had when she had heard the two of them conversing in the hall after dinner on Boxing Day.

Why were they so familiar with each other?

"Madam," she began, "or, Mama, I mean – "

"I think the less we hear from you now, Aurora, the better," hissed Lady Hartnell in an icy voice.

"But please – Mama – I must explain –"

Aurora felt her voice catching in her throat as she tried to tell her what had just taken place.

"I think that this will tell the tale quite adequately," smirked Lady Hartnell, as she raised the ripped silk skirt so that Aurora could see it clearly.

"You may well be skulking behind the sofa but you cannot hide from me that you are in a state of *undress*!"

"Please, Mama – "

Aurora tried to speak again, but Lady Hartnell just turned away from her.

"So, Robert," she asked with a supercilious smile, "how went the campaign?"

"She drew blood!" he moaned, nursing his hand.

"Just a mere scratch," laughed Lady Hartnell, and tossed the silk skirt at him, "and it seems you have given more than you got."

Lord Moreton scowled.

"She is a hellcat, Charlotte, and I have not had my way with her."

Lady Hartnell laughed again.

"Poor Robert. I should have left you to it for a little longer, but I was afraid that the entire household would be roused by your racket and I did not want the footmen and the butler bursting in with pitchforks and buckets of water to pull you both apart."

"Leave us then and let me finish what I came here for," snapped Lord Moreton. "I will not be denied!"

Aurora gasped with horror, as she felt the blood drain from her body at the thought of yet another onslaught from him.

She looked with despairing eyes at her stepmother, even though it was clear she was well aware of what had happened and did not seem at all angry with Lord Moreton.

Lady Hartnell smiled again and placed her hand on Lord Moreton's arm.

"Robert, Robert. Calm yourself. I think you have done more than enough."

She took up the large piece of torn skirt from where it had fallen when she had thrown it at him and folded it up carefully into a small square, tucking it into her waistband.

"Mama!" Aurora cried out and ran across to Lady Hartnell, desperate to explain what had occurred. "I begged him to leave."

"Be quiet now, Aurora, you are a perfect disgrace, you little minx. Just how dare you cavort in front of me in your petticoats? Where is your sense of respectability?"

"But – " Aurora stammered.

"Look at you! Enticing this poor gentleman, who you have recently rejected and insulted, into your clutches once again!"

Lady Hartnell pursed her lips into an expression of great disapproval.

"I think you must have *no* shame at all."

And she turned back to Lord Moreton and gave him a swift wink and a little sly smile.

Lord Moreton looked puzzled and seemed about to contradict Lady Hartnell, but then he suddenly smiled too and wiped the drops of blood from his hand onto his coat.

"Yes," he lisped, "shameless is the right word. She could not wait to get her claws into me."

"I – it – wasn't like that – "

Aurora could feel herself about to burst into tears as she struggled to defend herself.

Lord Moreton interrupted,

"Oh, Charlotte. If you could have seen the way she hurled herself at me. She was so violent in her passion she threw me to the floor!"

Lady Hartnell laughed again, this time very loudly and for a long time.

"I should like to have seen that," she said, when she had gained control of herself, "but one thing is very clear, my dear Robert. This young lady must be married as soon as possible, for she is clearly a liability both to herself and to others."

Lord Moreton nodded.

"Yes, indeed. My dear Charlotte, that would be a most satisfactory outcome for both of us."

Aurora then looked from one to the other of them in bewilderment.

"But I told Papa – "

"Your Papa, my dear Aurora," said Lady Hartnell, frowning at her and speaking once again in a cold precise voice, "would be most troubled to hear of your shocking and immoral behaviour this evening."

"But it was not my doing! I did not invite this man into my room – I tried to keep him out."

"Don't lie to me, you wicked creature. You turned down this delightful and charming man and then when you realised how much you were throwing away, you were so desperate to regain your dominion over him that you even had to resort to flaunting yourself in front of him in your petticoats!"

"No! No! It was *he* who tore my skirt!"

Lady Hartnell clicked her teeth in disdain.

"And what will your dear father say, do you think, if he discovers you were so desperate in your ungoverned passion to keep Lord Moreton in thrall to you that when your other wiles did not work, you sank your teeth into his flesh?"

"I will tell him – the truth – "

"And of course, Aurora, he will believe you, rather than listening to the evidence of his own dear wife and his dear friend and neighbour, Lord Moreton."

Lady Hartnell pursed her lips in disdain.

"I don't think that will be the case, do you, young lady?"

Her stepmother's sharp voice drilled into Aurora's head and made her feel sick and dizzy until the whole room seemed to be spinning around her.

She staggered backwards and dropped onto the sofa shaking with fear and shock.

"So I believe we have reached a most satisfactory conclusion," said Lady Hartnell. "The evening has gone so very well indeed."

"What – what – do you mean?" whispered Aurora.

"What I mean, young lady, is that there will be no more nonsense from you. It is more than clear from what has happened tonight that you obviously cannot be trusted to behave yourself.

"One moment you will accept this charming man's proposal and the next you are saying you reject him, only then to throw yourself at him in the most unbecoming and immoral fashion."

And she then turned her gaze on Lord Moreton as if expecting him to say something.

"Such inconsistency is very baffling indeed," lisped Lord Moreton, returning Lady Hartnell's glance.

He turned to Aurora.

"And yet, Miss Hartnell, in spite of your appalling behaviour, I still find it in myself to forgive you."

"Oh, come, Robert!" said Lady Hartnell with a little laugh. "You don't mean to tell me you will still have her?"

Lord Moreton gave his little squeaking laugh.

"And who else would, I wonder, after the events of this evening?"

"Indeed, Robert. We are agreed that the betrothal is just as it was and the wedding will go ahead as we planned.

The sooner that this young woman is safely married and under your roof the better!"

Aurora tried to rise to her feet and protest, but she was trembling too much, she could not force a word out.

Lady Hartnell turned and swept from the room and Lord Moreton followed her, looking back at Aurora with a strange expression that seemed to be half-triumph and half-greedy expectation.

She shuddered and shrank back on the sofa.

Her head ached and her arms hurt from where Lord Moreton had manhandled her, but far worse than that, her whole being felt soiled and besmirched.

Why had he come to her room when he knew that Papa was under the same roof, even though he had retired to his bed?

And more worryingly still, why had Lady Hartnell followed him and why had she refused to believe Aurora, or even listen to her explanation?

She had never felt so alone or so afraid in her life.

She longed for Phyllis to come and bathe her face and her bruised arms and lay out her nightgown on the bed.

But where was Phyllis?

She must have been gone for more than two hours.

Could it be that Phyllis too had turned against her?

Had she come back upstairs from the kitchen and seen or heard something she had misinterpreted?

Too shaken and frightened to undress and terrified that now she was completely and utterly alone in the world, Aurora crept into her bed and wept bitterly, her many tears soaking into the soft feather pillows.

CHAPTER SEVEN

Aurora slept at last, exhausted from the horrors of the night, but it seemed that no sooner had she closed her eyes and drifted away into merciful oblivion, than she was disturbed by a soft tapping noise.

She sprang awake and sat bolt upright in her bed, clutching her pillow and peering around the room that was now faintly visible through the grey dawn light.

The single candle had long gone out, leaving a pool of wrinkled wax on the table.

"Who is it?" she whispered, her voice sticking in her throat. "Phyllis, is that you?"

The tapping noise continued and Aurora realised it was coming from outside her window.

She stifled a scream at the awful thought that Lord Moreton had somehow managed to climb up the drainpipe and was crouching outside on the windowsill, knocking on the glass to attract her attention.

She lay back on the pillows, her heart pounding and waited for him to come crashing through the casement and resume his attack on her.

But nothing happened.

The tapping continued in a steady rhythm.

'It cannot be him,' she mused, breathing deeply and trying to calm her beating heart, 'he is much too drunk to be able to climb up the side of the Hall, and anyway, the drainpipe would never hold his weight.'

But what could the noise be?

There was something familiar and almost soothing about it as Aurora lay still and listened.

Suddenly she smiled to herself.

Of course, it was the sound of water dripping onto the windowsill from melting icicles.

She crept out of bed and went over to the window, lifting up the curtain to peer out and for a moment feeling a thrill of fear at the thought of seeing Lord Moreton's red face pressed against the glass.

But there was no one there.

The trees in the Park were veiled in thick fog and the snow was grey and dank, and starting to melt in places so that patches of dark earth showed through.

Aurora shivered and went over to sit at her dressing table.

Her cheeks felt raw from her hot tears and her body was bruised and stiff.

She was just picking up her brush to try and smooth her tangled hair when there was a scratch at the door.

Aurora leapt to her feet, seizing her heavy silver-backed mirror to use as a weapon.

The scratching came again and then the door inched open, revealing a white face with two black eyes peering warily out from under a white lace cap.

"Phyllis! Whatever happened to you?"

"Oh, Miss Aurora," sighed Phyllis. "Just wait till you hear what I have to tell!"

She slipped through the door and closed it behind her, leaning against it to ensure it was firmly shut.

And then she saw Aurora's torn dress and tangled hair and her eyes grew even larger and rounder.

"But Miss Aurora, whatever has happened to *you*!" I never saw such a sight in all my life."

"Oh, Phyllis!" cried Aurora, as tears welled up in her eyes again. "I don't know how to begin to tell you. If only you had been here."

Phyllis ran across the room and put her arms around Aurora.

"Phyllis, you are freezing!" she exclaimed, as she felt the icy touch of her maid's cold hands and the damp chill that clung to her clothes.

"Wherever have you been?"

Phyllis shook her head forlornly, as if she just could not believe what had happened to her.

"I went down to the kitchen, just as you told me to and cook had made a really fine dinner of beef stew with dumplin's.

"They were all sat around the kitchen table laughin' and jokin' and so I thought there would be no harm to sit down with them for a moment and eat my share."

"But, of course, Phyllis, I would expect you to do that."

"And while I was eatin', cook suddenly jumped to her feet like she'd seen a ghost and when I looked round, there was Lady Hartnell in all her finery standin' there at the kitchen door."

"But why? If she wanted to speak to cook, why did she not send for her to go to the drawing room?"

"Indeed. Poor cook, I felt she would have a heart attack from the colour she went. She thought she had done somethin' terribly wrong, but her Ladyship took no notice of cook. She came right into the kitchen and she stood by Frank the young footman and tapped him on the shoulder."

"Why, I think I saw her speaking to him yesterday, at the foot of the stairs. He has fair hair, hasn't he?"

"Yes, that is him. He has not been here very long. He got up and followed her out of the kitchen, and as she went out, Lady Hartnell turned back and looked at me, and my blood ran cold, for I didn't like what I saw in her eyes."

"Poor Phyllis," Aurora shivered, "I know that look very well."

"I finished my dinner and I asked cook if I might go to the pantry and find some things to bring for you and she told me where I could find the nicest morsels of cheese and the freshest bread."

"And I was here, waiting for you. So why did you not come?"

"I went out of the kitchen and down them steps into the pantry and I was just layin' out the tray for you when I heard footsteps comin' after me. I turned round, thinkin' it might be cook, and someone took hold of me and threw a blanket over my head!"

"Who was it?"

"I don't know, because I couldn't see a thing, but I think it must have been a man as he was very strong. I felt him take the tray from me and I fought to get away, but he twisted that rough old blanket round my head and my body so I couldn't hardly move.

"And then he just picked me up and carried me into somewhere cold and damp and threw me down on a stone floor."

"Were you hurt, Phyllis?"

"Why no, Miss Aurora, I was shocked, but I come to no harm. I heard a door shut and a bolt being drawn and then I threw off the blanket and looked around and I nearly passed out, for all around me there were great dead beasts and birds hangin' upside down and starin' at me with their bulgin' eyes!"

"Oh, poor Phyllis, you were locked up in the game larder!"

"Yes, Miss Aurora, and very cold and unpleasant it was too!"

Aurora shuddered at the thought of her maid lying on the damp floor surrounded by all the dead creatures.

And then she asked Phyllis if it could have been Frank who had locked her in the game larder.

"I don't rightly know for certain, miss, but it could have been. Why ever would he want to do that to me?"

Aurora took her maid's hand and led her over to the sofa, where she sat her down and told her of the terrible events of the previous night.

"But Miss Aurora," exclaimed Phyllis as she heard the full story of Lord Moreton's behaviour and about how Lady Hartnell had refused to believe her innocence.

"Your Papa would never ever stand such goin's on under his roof!"

"I know, Phyllis," said Aurora, wondering how she could ever have thought that her maid might doubt her or turn against her.

"But I couldn't make her listen and I now think she may have wanted to keep you away, so that you could not help me."

Phyllis hugged her tightly and told her not to fear, that all would be sorted out as soon as Lord Hartnell knew the full story.

Then she rang the bell for the parlour maid to come and make up the fire so that they could get warm at last.

*

Aurora was feeling fearful throughout that morning that either Lord Moreton or Lady Hartnell would return to her room.

So she kept Phyllis closely by her side, but no one came to bother her, and shortly before luncheon they saw Lord Moreton ride down the drive, sitting lopsidedly on a big brown horse.

"He has gone!"

Aurora turned to Phyllis.

"And suddenly I have got my appetite back. Let us ring down for some soup, as really I don't think I can face my stepmother just yet. I need to see Papa on his own."

As Phyllis ordered their luncheon from the parlour maid, Aurora sat back on the sofa, deeply relieved that her tormentor was no longer at Hadleigh Hall.

She looked out over the Park where the snow was now melting fast, uncovering large areas of green grass.

All of a sudden her heart skipped a beat.

Another horseman was rapidly approaching through the misty rain, spray from the wet grass flying up under his horse's hooves.

"Phyllis. Look, perhaps we have rejoiced too soon. Could that be Lord Moreton returning?"

Phyllis peered over her shoulder.

"No, Miss Aurora, most definitely not. Look what a gallop he comes at and how well he sits on his horse."

Aurora turned to speak to her, but Phyllis had gone from her side and was running towards the bedroom door.

"Where are you going?" she asked, alarmed at the secretive expression on her maid's face.

"I've got somethin' to attend to, miss. I'll be back before you know I have gone and I will be ever so careful not to speak to anyone carryin' a blanket!"

Aurora's heart sank as she now found herself alone again and she felt fearful at the nasty thought that Phyllis had deserted her and gone running off on a secret errand.

After a few minutes there was a light tap at the door and Aurora pulled the heavy silk cover from her bed and wrapped it around herself for protection.

"Who is it?" she called out and then felt ashamed of herself for being so afraid as she heard the parlour maid's whispered reply.

It was only the tray of soup for her luncheon.

"Where is my maid, Phyllis? Have you seen her downstairs?" she demanded and was surprised to see the parlour maid blushing and as if she was about to giggle.

"Yes, miss, I have," replied the girl, "she ran out of the house and I then saw her talkin' to a young man by the entrance to the stable yard."

The parlour maid grinned and then clapped a hand over her mouth as she realised that she had said more than she should.

Aurora felt faint with fear that Phyllis might have walked into another trap, or even worse, have betrayed her Mistress in some unforeseen way.

She waved for the parlour maid to leave and racked her brains to think what might be going on.

The luncheon tray was still lying untouched when Phyllis's light step was heard on the landing and she came skipping into the bedroom with a little smile on her face.

"Where have you been, Phyllis? How could you leave me alone after what I went through last night?"

"I'm sorry, Miss Aurora," admitted Phyllis, but she did not look at all remorseful and indeed seemed as if she might at any moment start dancing round the room.

"Who were you talking to by the stable yard? Don't lie to me Phyllis, I know that's where you have been. And what is that you are holding?"

She had suddenly noticed that Phyllis was carrying an envelope in her hand.

"You have been having an assignation with a man, the parlour maid saw you and he has passed notes to you."

Aurora felt so shocked that she could scarcely get her words out.

Much to her horror, Phyllis laughed out loud when she heard this, but before her Mistress could berate her for her brazen behaviour, she held out an envelope.

"You are right, Miss Aurora, but before you lay any blame where there be none, I think you should look at the name on this letter."

Aurora took the envelope and turned it over in her hands, feeling the luxurious texture of the heavy paper and then she caught her breath as she read her own name.

"*Miss Aurora Hartnell,*" written in a bold hand.

"Why, it's for me," she exclaimed.

"Yes, it is indeed and shame on you, Miss Aurora, for doubting my good conduct."

As she touched the fine black letters that spelled out her name, Aurora felt a shiver of excitement pass through her and it seemed that the envelope was filled with a warm glowing radiance so that she hardly dared to open it.

She looked out of the window for a second and saw the raindrops on the glass and the green Parkland emerging from the snow and ice and once again she heard the words the Earl had spoken to her as they bade each other farewell through the falling snow,

"*I shall send for you just as soon as the snow has melted.*"

She turned to Phyllis.

"This is from the Earl, isn't it? But how did you know? Was it him we saw riding through the Park?"

And she felt her heart pounding at the thought that he might have been so near to her.

"No, Miss Aurora, that wasn't him – there would be no mistakin' the Earl and his big black horse."

Phyllis went pink and bashful as she explained,

"The Earl had sent his coachman, Duncan, with the note. You might remember that I spoke with him when we were at Linford Castle."

Now it was Aurora's turn to laugh.

"Yes, I do, now that you come to mention it. He must have made quite an impression on you, Phyllis."

Phyllis's blush turned from a pink to a red and she looked uncomfortable.

"Yes, Miss Aurora. I just had a feelin' it might be him, when I saw the rider comin' through the Park and so I went down to see."

"I am so glad that you did, Phyllis."

Aurora turned to the light from the window to read the note.

As she went to open the envelope she noticed that the red wax seal on the back of it bore the outline of a little prancing unicorn, which must have come from the Earl's signet ring as she broke the red wax gently being careful to leave the impression intact.

She read through the polite and formal phrases with which the Earl began his letter and then felt her face grow warm with excitement,

"*It would give me great joy, Miss Hartnell, to share your company once more and to return to you a little of the pleasure you have given to me by bringing your delightful presence to Linford Castle.*

At the White Hart Inn, *an ancient hostelry which lies in a secluded spot on the banks of the river, there is a*

private dining room and the proprietor assures me that he will spare no effort to serve us there with the finest dinner in the County.

Will you meet with me tomorrow evening? I know, as I think I said to you when last we met, that your maid and amanuensis will be an admirable chaperone and if you are concerned that we may be seen at the inn, why not let's add to the delight of the evening with a little masquerade?

If you are agreeable, I shall meet with you there in the disguise of Jim the Carter, a respectable hard-working man, and perhaps you might care to reinvent yourself as Mary, his devoted wife?

If you would find pleasure in this gentle caper, it would be my privilege to be your host and rest assured that I would do everything in my power to assure your safety and enjoyment.

I await your reply with considerable anticipation and I remain, Miss Hartnell, your most devoted servant,

Linford."

Aurora folded the letter and held it against her heart for a moment, repeating softly to herself the last phrase of the letter, '*your most devoted servant*', as she conjured up the Earl's strong handsome face and eloquent dark eyes.

"What does it say, Miss Aurora?" enquired Phyllis, eagerly as she leant forward to see what was in the letter.

Aurora could not bear even for Phyllis to read the precious words the Earl had sent to her, but she told her of his request to meet her at the *White Hart Inn*.

"I would really love to go, Phyllis, but I really don't see how I can – "

"Why ever not?" countered Phyllis at once, "he is a true gentleman of noble heart and if I am to go with you and look out for you, I really can't see no harm in it."

"How do you know that we can trust him?" asked Aurora, a sudden chill striking her as she remembered Lord Moreton's cruel and unexpected onslaught last night.

"I feel it in my bones, miss, he has an honest face. And his servant speaks well of him and most truly means what he says, I'm quite sure."

Aurora noticed that Phyllis had gone slightly pink again and a sudden suspicion occurred to her.

"Phyllis! Are you quite sure you are not persuading me to go on this assignation simply so that you can have another tryst with Duncan?"

Phyllis coughed and looked embarrassed.

"I won't deny, miss, that I should be pleased to see that young man again, but it be yourself I'm a-thinkin' of. You deserve a little pleasure and do remember the kindness of that Earl in bringin' us home in that awful snowstorm."

Aurora read the letter again and sat for a while on the sofa trying to decide what she should do.

Should she go on such a wild adventure with this man she scarcely knew and yet whom she felt increasingly close to – this man who had invited her to his Castle and shared with her the sadness of his family history?

"I should not go without speaking to my Papa," she said, suddenly feeling remorseful. "I need to see him and explain what happened last night and then tell him what I am planning to do."

Phyllis looked sad.

"He is resting, Miss Aurora, I asked after him when I went to the stables and the butler said he was unwell and would not be receivin' any visitors today."

"Poor Papa," Aurora sighed, "he is never very well these days. I wish I could do more to make him feel better. But whenever I see him I just seem to add to his troubles."

She closed her eyes for a brief moment and tried to imagine her dear Mama sitting beside her on the sofa.

'What shall I do, Mama?' she pleaded, 'I just don't know which way to turn.'

But there was no reply to her silent question.

Instead she felt a warm glow inside herself, a gentle happiness that was like a deep echo of the feeling she had experienced when she read the Earl's letter.

She opened her eyes and turned to Phyllis.

"Fetch me some paper and a pen. I shall accept the Earl's invitation to go to the *White Hart Inn*. Just like you, Phyllis, I feel certain that the Earl is a good man and that Papa would want me to be happy and enjoy myself."

*

The next day Aurora tried several times to speak to her Papa, but his door remained firmly closed and his valet sent her away with a polite rebuff. He sent her his warm regards, but he was not well enough to receive her today.

Much to her relief Lady Hartnell kept a low profile as well and merely smiled at her coldly when they passed each other on the stairs.

Aurora and Phyllis took their meals in the bedroom and made their plans with great anticipation.

Phyllis spoke to a stable boy, who promised to get a pony and trap ready for them, as the Governess cart would be too recognisable.

In addition cook handed her a bundle of old clothes as she had grown too large for all her Sunday best dresses, but had never been able to throw them away.

"She didn't want to let them go, but I told her she should let me have them for charity for the poor folk in the village," explained Phyllis, as she laid out a pile of brown and grey woollen dresses and knitted shawls on the carpet.

"Then when we have finished with them, we must make sure they are all given away just as you promised."

Aurora held up one of the grey dresses on herself, and burst out laughing,

"Why this is far too big for me. I'm sure the Earl is not expecting to dine with an elephant!"

Phyllis frowned and rummaged through the pile.

"Do try this one, miss, its colour is more lavender than grey and we can drape a shawl around you so no one will be able to see how loose the waist is on you."

The sun was now beginning to set and darkness was creeping over the Park as the two of them completed their dressing.

Aurora became the perfect carter's wife in a dark brown shawl tucked over the lavender dress, but even the addition of a large white cap to hide her auburn hair could not hide the fact that under the heavy layers of clothing there was a young and attractive girl with a slim figure.

"Is it time to go?" Aurora asked, suddenly feeling nervous as she watched Phyllis putting on a white country woman's cap and wrapping a big grey shawl round herself.

"Yes, indeed, miss, the trap will be waitin' for us down in the stable yard."

Aurora folded the Earl's note and tucked it into the knot at the front of her shawl and the two of them crept down the narrow backstairs, only used by the servants, and made their way out through the scullery door.

The kitchen maids were all busy at the scullery sink preparing vegetables for dinner and Aurora felt a thrill of fear as one of them looked up and caught her eye.

Aurora quickly turned away and adjusted the folds of the heavy shawl around her shoulders, hoping that the big white cap had kept her face hidden and that the girl had not recognised her.

The air outside was fresh and cold as they hurried through into the stable yard.

She could see the breath from the pony harnessed to the trap hanging in the air like a cloud of steam.

"We should go right away," said Aurora urgently, "I'm sure that girl knew who we were. What if she tells my stepmother's footman?"

"Don't worry, miss," whispered Phyllis, "look, they have tied the little pony's hooves in sackcloth, so no one will hear us when we leave."

Aurora gathered up her skirts and was just about to climb into the trap when she heard a dog barking loudly.

As she turned to see what was happening, the stable yard was suddenly filled with swinging lantern lights and she heard shouts and running feet and more loud barking.

"Quickly, Phyllis!" she cried, for she had caught a glimpse of a fair-headed young man in the flickering light, "*I think they are on to us!*"

Phyllis ran to join her, but fell to the ground as a large mastiff jumped at her and seized her arm in its jaws.

"Go on, Miss Aurora! Quickly!" she cried, twisting away from the dog as she tried to lift up her face from the cobblestones.

Aurora took the reins and tried to steer the trap out of the stable yard, but there, in the middle of the gateway, blocking her exit, was a tall silhouette dressed in full skirts and crowned with a feather.

It was Lady Hartnell.

CHAPTER EIGHT

There was no other way out of the stable yard.

Aurora was trapped.

Frank, the footman, ran up and grabbed Aurora by the arms, pulled her down from the pony trap and dragged her across the yard to where her stepmother stood waiting.

"So, who is this?" Lady Hartnell said imperiously. "Some kind of labourer's wife? What can such a person be doing at this time of night upon our premises?"

She reached out for the big white cap that covered Aurora's auburn curls and pulled it from her head.

"Ah, how interesting," she smiled coldly. "Let's see what your father has to say about this!"

Aurora looked round to see what was happening to Phyllis, as she could hear the big dog that had attacked her snarling and growling, but she was surrounded by a crowd of stable boys and was hidden from her view.

Lady Hartnell led the way to the front door of the house, her long skirts swishing over the gravel and Aurora followed behind shaking with fear.

What would Papa say?

How she wished that she had tried harder to speak to him and tell him the whole story about Lord Moreton's shocking behaviour the previous night and her plan to meet with the Earl for dinner that night.

Papa had risen from his bed and was now seated in a chair at the foot of the stairs.

As soon as they entered the hall, he pulled himself to his feet holding out a piece of paper in his shaking hand.

"What can be the meaning of this?" he croaked, his voice choking with anger.

"Have you *no* shame at all? No sooner has my dear Charlotte informed me that you have regretted your callous attitude to Lord Moreton and agreed to accept him after all than you plot this wicked escapade behind my back!"

And he thrust the paper into her face.

It was the Earl's letter.

Aurora felt the blood draining from her head as she realised that she must have dropped the Earl's letter in the scullery when she was adjusting the folds of her shawl.

"Papa – there has been a – misunderstanding – "

"Indeed there has, I have completely misunderstood you. Your untrustworthiness knows no bounds."

Aurora saw with distress that his face was turning dark red and his whole body was trembling.

And it was all because of her.

Somehow she just had to find a way to make him comprehend what had really happened.

Stammering and blushing she tried hard to explain the sequence of events of the night before.

"I don't need to hear any of this," he exploded. "I have heard from Charlotte exactly what occurred last night and how you lured Lord Moreton into your room."

"No, Papa! He tricked me and forced his way into my room. I haven't agreed to marry him, that is the truth!"

"Listen to her," snarled Lady Hartnell. "Now she is trying to tell us she has changed her mind again!"

"Perhaps I might have believed you," he sighed, his voice suddenly weary. "Were it not for this – "

He waved the letter at her again.

"Ah, yes!" Lady Hartnell smiled, "a young woman who will agree to meet a man in secret – and in disguise – is a young woman whose word can most definitely not be trusted."

"That is indeed so."

Lord Hartnell then lowered himself slowly into the chair again.

"Have you put in motion what we agreed, my dear Charlotte?"

He looked at Lady Hartnell.

"Indeed I have," she replied. "You, miss, had better go to your room and pack your things. You are going to be sent away for a spell."

"Where?" cried Aurora, feeling cold with shock.

"A place where you can be kept quiet and out of the way until you are safely married," added Lady Hartnell.

"But where is Phyllis?" demanded Aurora, trying to keep her voice from trembling. "I will need her to help me pack and she must go with me, of course, I cannot manage – without her."

"I have given orders for her to be locked up in the cellar to reflect on her bad behaviour," said Lady Hartnell.

"But none of this is in any way Phyllis's fault. It's most unfair."

Lord Hartnell was struggling onto his feet again.

"It may well be that the maid has been corrupted by my daughter," he declared, shaking his head sadly. "But Phyllis looked after my former wife and has always been a servant of excellent character. Let her out from the cellar, Charlotte, and send them both away together. I don't want *either of them* under my roof anymore."

He turned and began to climb up the stairs slowly, pulling himself up by the banisters.

Lady Hartnell followed and took hold of his elbow, impatiently trying to hurry him along.

Aurora watched them with tears running down her face until she heard a commotion behind her in the hall.

"There ain't no need to shove me around like that," came a pert West Country voice. "I've a pair of legs and I am well able to walk!"

It was Phyllis.

Frank had her by the arm and was pushing her into the hall. Aurora was horrified to see that Phyllis's sleeve was torn and ragged and her dress wet and dirty.

"Are you all right?" she asked, hastily wiping her face so that Phyllis should not see she had been crying.

"I am sorely bruised, miss, where that mastiff took hold of me and likely to be more bruised, if *this* young dog will not leave go!"

She scowled fiercely at Frank.

"What will become of me?" whispered Aurora, as they crept up the stairs with Frank following close at their heels.

"I don't know, miss," responded Phyllis. "We must pack our bags and hope for the best, that's all I can say."

Aurora could not put her mind to packing at all and Phyllis ran round the bedroom opening up endless drawers and wardrobes and flinging garments into a couple of large holdalls, while her Mistress sat on her bed, trying hard to control her racing thoughts.

What would the Earl think of her, when she did not appear at the inn?

Aurora felt her eyes filling with tears again as she thought of him waiting for her in the private dining room at the *White Hart Inn*, and pictured the expression in his eyes as he looked up and saw her walking through the door.

The picture was so real that for a minute she forgot her desperate situation.

'Why am I not frantically worried over what is now going to happen to me?' she asked herself. 'Why can I only think about the Earl, this man I hardly know and may never see again?'

Suddenly the door was pushed open abruptly and Lady Hartnell entered, a cynical smile on her face.

"Come, miss," she sneered. "Your carriage awaits you. Why, what a fright you look!"

Aurora was still wearing cook's dress and shawl, but she did not care how she might appear.

She allowed herself to be led back down the stairs, and out of the front door, Phyllis following behind with the heavy holdalls.

A closed carriage with the blinds pulled down was outside the front door drawn by two excited horses, which were tossing their heads and pawing the gravel.

Numb to everything Aurora allowed Lady Hartnell to push her through the door of the carriage.

She fell onto the leather seat, landing awkwardly against the bulky body of someone sitting inside.

A strong odour of cigars stung Aurora's nose.

It could only be Lord Moreton.

Lady Hartnell slammed the carriage door and then tapped on the window.

Lord Moreton leaned across and lifted the blind.

"Robert. There can be no further obstacles to our plan."

Her voice was somewhat muffled by the glass.

"Success is ours, if *you* keep your nerve."

Lord Moreton uttered a squeaking laugh and let the blind drop, as he turned his attention to his passenger.

Aurora had no time to cry out in protest before she felt the carriage rocking violently.

They were on their way.

"So," lisped Lord Moreton, as he pulled a cigar out of his coat pocket. "*I have you at last!*"

"You cannot do this," Aurora stammered. "I do not – consent to go – with you."

"You will come to no harm, my dear," he hissed, snipping the end off his cigar and lighting it. "You will be very safe at Elton Hall, until such time as we are married."

"I will never marry you!" cried Aurora, choking as Lord Moreton breathed a cloud of thick cigar smoke at her.

Desperate for air, she seized the leather strap of the carriage window and pulled it down.

Lord Moreton's heavy body bore down upon her as he leaned across to pull up the window again and Aurora shuddered as she felt his hands gripping her shoulders.

He pressed her down to the floor, and, gripping the cigar between his teeth, he pulled the emerald necklace out of his pocket and fastened it roughly round her neck.

Aurora twisted and turned, desperate to free herself, and managed to catch Lord Moreton in the belly with the point of her elbow.

He shouted out as he writhed in pain and, as they struggled together, Aurora felt the red-hot tip of his cigar brush her neck.

She screamed in agony from the burn, and then she and her attacker fell onto the floor, crushed into the small space between the seats.

The carriage was swinging from side to side, so that first Lord Moreton and then Aurora were thrown against the doors.

Aurora screamed again, and very faintly, from the coachman's seat above, she heard Phyllis's voice calling her name.

Suddenly the carriage lurched to an abrupt halt.

Aurora heard the shrill neighing of a horse and then there was a splintering crash and she found herself lying on top of Lord Moreton as the carriage then tipped over onto its side.

There was a gust of cold damp air and a spatter of raindrops in her face as the door opened.

"Quick, Miss Aurora!" called out Phyllis. "Get out now!"

She scrambled to her feet, cringing as she felt her boots trampling over Lord Moreton's flesh and then hauled herself out of the door.

As she emerged from the carriage door, it was as if someone had thrown a bucket of water in her face.

"My goodness, it's pouring," she gasped, wrapping the woollen shawl around her head.

"Yes, Miss Aurora. Never mind that now. Get out quickly while you can. We've been held up!"

Phyllis caught her Mistress's hands to steady her.

As Aurora stepped down from the carriage and onto the ground, she saw in the flickering light from the carriage lantern, two horsemen across the road ahead, both mounted on big carthorses and wearing thick rough cloaks.

"Ho!" a man's voice called out loudly. "We have a damsel in distress!"

Aurora clutched at Phyllis's hand, shivering in the cold rain.

"What is going on? Are we to be abducted again?"

The taller of the two horsemen dug his heels into the sides of his mount and approached them.

His face was smeared with dirt and as he swept his broad-brimmed hat off in a mock salute, the rain plastering his wild dark hair flat against his head.

"May I be of service to you, ladies?" he said. "For your carriage, I fear, is wrecked!"

Aurora looked round and saw that the vehicle was indeed badly damaged, as it lay on its side in the ditch, with the coach horses struggling to regain their feet in the sticky mud as the coachman pulled at their tangled reins.

"I think they mean us no harm," muttered Phyllis, as she looked anxiously at the two mysterious horsemen in the road.

But no sooner had she spoken than there was a roar of wild rage from the shattered carriage and Lord Moreton emerged, arms waving like a windmill.

Aurora backed away from him at once and then she realised that she was standing right by the stirrup of the tall man who had held up their carriage.

She was caught just there in the middle of the road between the two of them.

"Just what in the name of hell is going on?" Lord Moreton blustered, gesticulating at the horsemen. "Who are you, and how dare you interrupt our journey like this! Look what you have done to my carriage."

"Sir," answered the taller man in a country accent, "it's a very dark night and the road is slippery. As we came round the bend your horses took fright and tipped you into the ditch. It was plain bad luck, sir, and no fault of ours."

"That's as maybe," growled Lord Moreton, "but I will see that you pay for this, you blackguards. You have no business to be terrorising innocent travellers."

"Do you call yourself a gentleman, sir?" the tall man retorted. "Look to your ladies – would you leave them standing in the road on a night like this?"

He swung his horse around and reached down to Aurora, holding out his hand to her.

"Come on sweetheart," he called down. "Jump up behind me and I will soon have you safe and warm."

Something in his voice made Aurora shiver.

He sounded strangely familiar to her in spite of his odd accent.

She looked at the heavy rain-spattered leather glove he was wearing and suddenly she wanted to reach out and grasp his hand, letting him swing her up behind him on his sturdy horse.

"My fiancée is not a concern of yours, you devil," Lord Moreton hissed. "Get back over here, you minx!"

And he lurched across the road to try and grab her.

Aurora sprang away from him, clutching the shawl, which was now soaking wet, around herself.

"You let her be!" shouted the horseman. "She wants none of you, it's clear."

He turned his horse to block Lord Moreton's way.

"I'll bring you to heel, you little madam," shouted Lord Moreton.

He went back to the wrecked carriage and seized the coachman's long whip, waving it wildly at Aurora.

She jumped, trying to dodge out of the way and lost her footing, falling in the mud.

"Enough!" the horseman yelled, leaping down from the saddle and in an instant he was grappling with Lord Moreton, pulling the whip from his hand and throwing it into the ditch.

Aurora heard Phyllis scream out and she saw for an instant in the dull lamplight the gleam of a metal blade in Lord Moreton's hand.

She struggled to her feet and felt the shawl falling back from her head and the cold rain beating down on her.

"Careful," she shouted to the horseman. "He has a knife!"

Lord Moreton lunged forward, but the other man was too quick for him and like lightning, seized his wrist and twisted it – and at the same time kicking forward and knocking Lord Moreton's feet from under him, so that he fell heavily into the ditch.

The horseman chuckled, shaking the rain from his hair and turned to Aurora.

"Now, sweetheart!" he called, "what is your wish?"

He took a step towards her, holding out his gloved hands and then suddenly stopped in his tracks.

His dirt-smeared face gleamed in the rain and his eyes looked wild as the lamplight caught them.

Aurora backed away.

"*It's you!*" he breathed and reached out for her.

"No!" cried Aurora, suddenly terrified that she was about to be attacked again. "Keep away from me!"

"*Do you not know me?*"

Aurora wiped the rain out of her eyes, desperately trying to think how she could avoid this dishevelled rough man who seemed determined to take hold of her.

But he seemed to have noticed that she was afraid, and had halted just a few feet away.

"Miss Hartnell," he said in a gentle voice with not a trace of a rough accent, "what is going on?"

It was the Earl.

She had not recognised him in these working man's clothes and with a dirty face – in full dress for their secret assignation at the *White Hart Inn*.

Aurora struggled to find her voice, but she could not even raise a whisper and stood shivering, cold and wet, in the middle of the road.

"I wondered why you did not come tonight," the Earl was saying, "for I received your letter assenting to our meeting and I was sure that you were a lady of your word. I am on my way back to Linford Castle and now I find you like this."

"I – I – " she gasped, but still she could not speak and even if she could have made a sound, she would not have known what to say to him.

He was gazing intently at her, all the wildness and roughness gone and as she met his dark ardent eyes, she felt flooded with warmth despite the freezing rain.

"Why did you not come?" he asked her softly.

"I – would – I was – " she whispered and held out the old woollen shawl, now soaking with rain, that she had been wearing, so that he could see her disguise.

But before the Earl could make out what she was trying to say, there was a noise of splashing and grunting, as Lord Moreton rose from the flooded ditch and staggered over to them.

"So," he spluttered, "Linford! The rascal who has been trying to poach my fiancée!"

"You mind your words," the Earl retorted, his brow creased with anger.

"But I have put a stop to your little game," snorted Lord Moreton. "She is safely mine at last."

The Earl turned to Aurora.

"What is this, Miss Hartnell? You did not tell me you were engaged."

"I am *not*," she spluttered, finding her voice at last.

"The faithless little vixen!" howled Lord Moreton, and gave his unpleasant high-pitched laugh. "So fickle and wayward, she doesn't even know her own mind."

He grabbed the emerald necklace roughly so that the stones cut into Aurora's neck, choking her.

"She says she will have me and accepts my gifts – look at these stones. They don't come cheap, I will have you know, and then throws them back in my face – "

"Miss Hartnell, is this true?"

The Earl's frown was deepening.

"I – it – " she stammered, praying that the necklace would break and free her throat. "I made a bad – mistake."

"Yes!" cried Lord Moreton. "And then, the trollop, she realises what she has lost in rejecting me and entices me back into her clutches by most devious and unladylike means."

Lord Moreton gave the necklace a final twist and then released it, pushing Aurora roughly so that she fell to her knees on the muddy road.

"But this is the woman who is to be my wife," he continued in a calmer voice, "so I shall speak no further of her treacherous and deceitful character."

The Earl looked down at Aurora but made no move to help her up.

"Far be it from me to come between a man and his wife-to-be," he sighed.

Aurora felt the necklace burning into the skin of her throat, stifling her words.

'It's like a slave's collar,' she thought. 'I will never be free of it.'

"Come, Duncan," the Earl was saying, "we must be on our way."

The second horseman had also dismounted and was coaxing Lord Moreton's frightened horses out of the ditch, watched by Phyllis still cowering under the hedge.

"Duncan!" the Earl raised his voice and the sound of it cut through Aurora like a knife.

Duncan then jumped from the ditch and pulled off his heavy cloak, which he tossed towards Phyllis.

He leapt onto his horse and taking the other one by the reins, led it over to the Earl.

'He believes Lord Moreton's lies. He is not even going to speak to me,' mused Aurora, as she watched the Earl swing into the saddle and dig his heels into the plump sides of his carthorse, 'not even to say 'goodbye'.'

The rain was beginning to slacken as she watched the two men ride away out of the circle of lamplight and disappear into the night.

She put her hands up to the emerald necklace and tried to undo it, but her fingers were too stiff with cold to work the clasp.

She tugged hard at it, but still it would not break.

'There is nothing I can do,' she thought, 'and there is no one who will help me. I must marry Lord Moreton – although I would rather *die* – '

She struggled onto her feet and then turned to face her future husband.

Soaked with the rain and covered in goblets of mud from the wet ditch, he seemed even less prepossessing than usual.

Aurora choked with utter misery as she gazed at his round heavy face and small puffy eyes and reflected that this was the sight she must now face every day for the rest of her life.

Suddenly there was a rustle behind Lord Moreton, and something heavy flew into the air and descended like a black cloud over his head.

Lord Moreton gave a muffled shout and flailed his arms around, but he was completely covered in the folds of a thick woollen cloak.

"Quick then, Miss Aurora," hissed Phyllis, peering round from behind him, her hair straggling and wet, "take this strap and help me tie him up."

She tossed a long piece of leather from the coach horses' harness at Aurora.

Lord Moreton was fighting hard to free himself.

But Phyllis, although only a fraction of his size and weight, skilfully twisted the folds of the cloak around him so that he had little room to move and in a few moments Aurora had him tightly strapped up.

He writhed and struggled and Aurora could hear his frantic bellows through the thick cloak.

Phyllis dragged him off the road and into the ditch again, where they left him next to his coachman, who had also been neatly tied up with pieces of harness and gagged with Phyllis's white cap.

"Now," crowed Phyllis, going over to the wrecked coach and untying their two holdalls from the rack on the roof.

"We'll sling these over one horse, and me being no sort of a rider, Miss Aurora, I'll sit up behind you on the other."

"But Phyllis – "

"No buts, Miss Aurora, we have no time to lose."

The two coach horses had been untangled and were now standing quietly under the hedge.

Phyllis and Aurora tied the heavy bags so that they lay across the back of one and then Aurora scrambled up onto the other.

It felt strange not to have a saddle, but the remains of the harness were there to cling onto.

"Come on, Phyllis, jump up," she urged.

"It's a long way from the ground," gasped Phyllis, shaking with fear as she climbed up by way of a tree stump in the hedge.

"Be brave, Phyllis, don't lose heart now, after what you have just done!"

Phyllis gave a little snort.

"Why, yes. I learned a trick or two from Frank the footman, didn't I?"

Aurora then remembered Duncan throwing her the cloak and was longing to ask what part he had just played in Lord Moreton's downfall, but she suddenly felt a deep shiver travel down her spine and knew that they must stay no longer.

"Where shall we go, Phyllis?" she asked.

"We shall go West, Miss Aurora," replied her maid. "To Cornwall!"

The road in front of them was dark and everything that Aurora knew and cared for was lost.

But then she could only hope and pray, as the horse bounded forward beneath her, that what lay ahead was no worse than what she was leaving behind.

CHAPTER NINE

Aurora lay in the small bedroom under the eaves at Treworra House and gazed out through the diamond-paned window towards the sea.

She could not remember how long she had been ill, but at last her fever had gone and she was beginning to feel a little better.

She thought feverously back over the long journey to Cornwall, recalling how Phyllis had taken that unlucky emerald necklace and been able to sell it in one of the little country towns they passed through.

It went for only a fraction of its worth, since no one would believe that those stones were real, but with a few coins in their pockets they were able to buy saddles for the coach horses and also pay for simple rooms at the inns and hostelries along their way.

And how useful cook's cast-off gowns had proved, although they had been the subject of much teasing and friendly ribaldry where they stayed.

But no one had questioned that the two women in the thick woollen dresses and heavy shawls were not Amy and Prudence, a carter's wife and her cousin, travelling to visit their family in Cornwall.

And eventually they had arrived here, at Phyllis's suggestion, at this delightful old house where Miss Morris, a childhood friend of Aurora's Mama, lived.

Grey-haired and gentle, Miss Morris had welcomed

them most kindly, saying it was a joy to see her old friend live again in the beauty of her daughter and that she was happy to be of service to Aurora in any way.

Aurora had endured being battered by cold and rain as they travelled the muddy roads and had not complained for an instant about the damp sheets and the bad food they encountered at some of the inns.

But the journey had taken its toll of her and as soon as she reached the safety of Miss Morris's house, she fell ill with chills and fever.

Miss Morris nursed her most tenderly, sitting up at all hours beside her bed and then concocting nourishing delicacies in case Aurora's appetite should return.

Now, as she lay looking out of the window, Aurora was alone.

In the distance she could hear Church bells ringing, so it must be Sunday morning and Miss Morris must have gone to the service.

Aurora stretched herself and sat up.

The room was warm and cosy and yet there was a sad feel to it.

It was rather like Miss Morris herself, she thought, who was dainty and kind and always looked immaculately clean and well-presented, but whose gentle grey eyes held a deep and resigned unhappiness.

Aurora shivered and wrapped the bed covers round her.

All the while she had been ill, she had not thought about the terrible events that had brought her to Cornwall for the pain had been too much for her to bear.

But now she was starting to feel stronger and more clear-headed and so she must face up to the reality of her predicament.

'I can never return home,' she reflected, 'my Papa will never accommodate me under his roof again and as for Lord Moreton, what would he do to me, if he was ever to see me again? *I am an outcast!*'

But there was one other even more painful thought that she must face up to.

And that was the fact that she would never be able to see the Earl again, hear his voice and see his dark eyes light up at the sight of her.

'He believes I am treacherous and fickle and every manner of bad things a woman might be,' she moaned to herself as she lay back on her soft pillows, a tear trickling down the side of her nose.

'And perhaps I am!'

There was a knock at the door and Phyllis entered, carrying a tray.

"Why there's an improvement," she burbled. "You be sittin' up, miss. But whatever is the matter?"

Aurora told her, as best she could, as she was now sobbing wildly and could hardly get her words out.

Phyllis laid the tray on the side table and sat down by the bed.

"Look here, miss" she said kindly. "I have brought you tea and the thinnest slices of bread and butter. Do try some, please – you haven't eaten a thing in so many days."

Aurora was feeling extremely weak, but she tried to calm her sobs and after she had sipped a little hot tea and tasted the bread and butter, she felt some vitality seeping back into her exhausted body.

"That is so good, Phyllis, but what am I going to do? I just don't know which way to turn."

"Well now, miss, you can't do anythin' but rest for the time bein', since you've been so very ill. But there is no need to worry, because Miss Morris has told me you are welcome to stay here for as long as you want. And as for the other business, well – you are in a fix and no mistake, but I am sure there'll be a way out of it."

Aurora smiled as somehow it was just impossible to feel gloomy in the company of Phyllis, who would never allow herself to be defeated by any situation.

After all even Lord Moreton had been no match for her!

"I should like a little more bread and butter, please, and then perhaps tomorrow I shall think about getting up."

"That's the spirit, Miss Aurora," enthused Phyllis and then she frowned.

"What is the matter?" Aurora asked her.

"There's just one thing that be botherin' me about us never bein' able to go back to Hadleigh Hall."

"What?" asked Aurora.

"Well, we never did find out what an '*amanuensis*' is and now we'll never be able to ask your father!"

Aurora burst out laughing.

"Oh Phyllis, you are so funny sometimes! Don't worry, I am sure Miss Morris will have a dictionary."

*

The next day, Aurora felt so much recovered that she was able to come downstairs and sit with Miss Morris in the parlour.

She sat by the fireside and watched Miss Morris's slender fingers pulling a needle through a piece of linen as she created a beautiful silk rose on a cushion cover.

"How are you feeling now, my dear?" Miss Morris asked in her soft gentle voice.

"I am much better, thank you, and I must thank you too so much for all your kindness to me."

"Why, it's a great pleasure to have my dear friend Marianne's daughter in my home," smiled Miss Morris.

"I don't know how much Phyllis has told you – "

"She has told me everything, as far as I know," said Miss Morris gravely and laid aside her embroidery. "You are in a difficult position, my dear, but I do not think that you have done anything wrong."

"Who will ever believe that, though? When Lord Moreton and Stepmother are telling such different stories?"

"That is where the difficulty lies, but we must place our trust in the Good Lord and the truth will prevail, I am sure of it. And you have a home with me here for as long as you need it."

Aurora sighed.

Although she was feeling warm and well-cared for and now sitting in a most comfortable armchair, she could not help but feel very sad and low.

She shook herself, realising that she was showing a great lack of manners.

"Thank you, dear Miss Morris, your kindness goes far beyond anything I could have expected. But may I ask you something?"

"Of course, Aurora."

"Do you know what an *amanuensis* is?"

Aurora experienced a sudden pain in her heart as she remembered the Earl's low voice saying the word, as they faced each other through the whirling snow.

Miss Morris laughed.

"What a strange question, my dear! I think it is a Latin word and means 'a special trusted servant', who will obey your every command, but where did you come across this word?"

"Phyllis will be very delighted," murmured Aurora, blushing and declining to answer Miss Morris's question, "I think she thought it might mean something derogatory."

"Not at all, my dear, a most appropriate use of the word is when it is applied to your wonderful Phyllis! But I can check that the meaning I have given you is correct. I will ask our Vicar, Mr. Bramley, when he comes to call."

Aurora thanked Miss Morris and was a bit surprised to note that as she spoke of the Vicar, a cloud of sadness passed her face.

"Are you all right, Miss Morris?" she asked.

"Yes, yes, of course. I must go and check that all is well with cook in the kitchen."

Miss Morris then hurriedly left the room.

Aurora felt a distinct tightness around her heart as she watched her leave as her charming hostess was clearly upset about something.

'I do wish I could speak to her about the Earl,' she reflected, 'but I dare not. It is a secret I cannot share with anyone.'

And hot tears filled her eyes, because she could not get the image of his strong handsome face out of her mind.

Suddenly she caught a movement in the corner of the room and saw a tall figure in a grey crinoline dress with an old-fashioned billowing skirt standing there.

Aurora then caught her breath, as she had not been aware that there was anyone else in the parlour.

"I am so sorry," she whispered, "I did not see you there. Who are you?"

The figure turned towards her.

It was a young woman with long fair hair looped back over her ears.

She moved silently towards the fireplace and then sat down opposite Aurora and bent over putting her head in her hands.

Aurora's ears were ringing and her pulses racing, so that she wondered for a moment if she was going to be ill again.

But the strange sensation she was feeling seemed in some way to be connected to the young woman in the old-fashioned dress.

"Are you all right?" she asked her, for the young woman seemed to be distressed.

She looked up and stared at Aurora with her wide grey eyes.

She did not open her mouth, but Aurora seemed to hear a voice ringing in her ears.

"He does not come. I wait and wait and the one I love does not come."

The voice echoed round inside Aurora's head and her vision blurred as the parlour grew dark and disappeared as she fell into a deep faint.

When Aurora awake from her faint she was lying in her bed and Miss Morris was leaning over her, her soft face creased with anxiety.

"My poor dear," she began gently, "you should not have got up so soon, you are still very unwell."

Aurora sat up, propping herself on her pillows. Her head felt clear and the sadness round her heart had melted away, leaving her feeling much stronger and brighter.

"Please don't trouble yourself, dear Miss Morris, I am really much better. I was just very surprised to see the other lady in your parlour. I was not expecting to meet her – and it was rather a shock."

Miss Morris shook her head.

"I don't know who you are referring to – I have had no visitors today."

"Oh, but she came over and spoke to me. A very pretty woman with fair hair tied back and wearing a grey dress – "

Miss Morris's face was normally pale, but now she turned as white as marble.

"What – what did she say to you?" she asked, her voice trembling.

"I think she said 'he does not come – the one I love does not come – ' She seemed to be very upset and I was about to comfort her when I fainted."

"Oh dear!"

Miss Morris pulled out her handkerchief and held it over her mouth to hide her trembling lips.

"It is *Emily*! Oh dear!"

"Who is Emily?" Aurora asked her, reaching out to take Miss Morris's hand.

"She is – she was – my dear elder sister. You have described her exactly."

Aurora felt a strange chill pass through her body.

"Has Emily – passed away?"

"Oh yes, my dear!"

She dabbed her eyes with her handkerchief.

"We lost her fifteen years ago, poor soul. And yet I often feel that she is still with me lingering in all the places she loved."

Aurora sat up and was about to put her arms around Miss Morris, but she moved back, as if she did not want to be comforted.

"Dear Emily," she was saying, "she did suffer so. She was betrothed, but her beloved Frederick died of his wounds out in the Crimea and after that she took no joy in life at all. She slowly lost her mind and I could not make her understand that he would not return."

"It is terrible to lose the one you love," said Aurora, feeling her own eyes watering.

"That is so," agreed Miss Morris, wiping her eyes and sitting up straight again on her bedside chair.

"And perhaps I am fortunate in my spinsterhood, as I have never had to suffer that terrible pain of loss."

Aurora did not know what to say.

Although it hurt her terribly to think that she would never see the Earl again, at least she had the memory of him and, even though it was painful, she could still feel the thrill of his presence when she recalled the sound of his voice and the look in his eyes.

Miss Morris was getting up to leave her, saying that Aurora must sleep soundly to recover her strength after her faint.

"You are still very weak and I am sure that is why you have been troubled by this vision. I will send for Mr. Bramley tomorrow morning and he will be able to give us some spiritual advice on the matter."

And again Aurora noticed sadness creep into Miss Morris's grey eyes.

'Oh, Mama,' she whispered, as she lay back against the soft feather pillows, 'I think there is something I must do here. This sadness is so very strong, but it feels like the unhappiness at Valley Farm. So do please help me, Mama, for I don't quite know what it is I should do – "

A feeling of gentle warmth ran through her veins, and she seemed to hear a soft voice whisper to her,

'*All will be well, and when the time comes, you will know what you must do.*'

Aurora sighed deeply.

She felt the tension and weariness dissolve from her body as she relaxed into a deep and healing sleep.

*

Next day the winter sun was shining in through the little diamond-paned window in her bedroom when Aurora awoke.

A tray of tea and toast lay on the bedside table and she realised she must have slept well past breakfast time.

She jumped out of bed, snatching a piece of toast to nibble on and went over to the window.

'I am now completely recovered,' she thought, 'my strength has come back.'

Miss Morris's garden was planted with all kinds of old-fashioned herbs and bushes.

There were no flowers, as it was still deep winter, but the plants were all trimmed into neat shapes and gave an impression of great peace and harmony.

Aurora saw a short slightly bowed man dressed in black approaching the garden gate.

'It must be Mr. Bramley, the Vicar,' she surmised, 'I must dress and go down.'

And she called for Phyllis to help her.

"I am so much better," she told her. "I feel I could run a mile!"

"Now that would be foolishness indeed," muttered Phyllis, as she fastened up the back of her dress. "And I for one would not be comin' with you."

When Aurora arrived downstairs, Mr. Bramley was seated in the parlour with Miss Morris, who was pouring coffee from an old silver pot.

He had a round red face, which reminded Aurora of a wrinkled apple with white hair as soft as thistledown.

'How kind he looks,' she decided, as he rose from his chair to greet her.

"Miss Hartnell." Mr. Bramley took her hand in his. "I am delighted to meet you. You are from Hadleigh Hall, in Dorset, I believe. By a strange coincidence, my cousin, Arthur, is Chaplain to the Earl of Linford, whose Castle I believe, is just a short ride away from Hadleigh Hall."

Aurora looked away, feeling her knees grow weak at the mere mention of the Earl's name.

Mr. Bramley released her hand and helped her to a chair.

Miss Morris told him about Aurora's illness and all about the episode the day before.

"Poor child, she seemed to see a vision of my sister Emily now long deceased, which must have been brought on by her weakness."

Mr. Bramley turned to Aurora.

"Were you very frightened by this, my dear?"

"No, I felt very sad but not frightened," she replied, looking into Mr. Bramley's kind blue eyes. "You see, this has happened to me before and I think it is something that happened to my Mama too."

She told Mr. Bramley of her experience with Ivy at Valley Farm and added,

"Sometimes, I believe, a person's spirit may linger, and not be able to move on – "

Mr. Bramley looked concerned.

"You paint a tragic picture, my dear, and indeed it is possible that a soul might remain earthbound and not be able to experience the miracle of Divine Love."

Miss Morris was holding her handkerchief over her face and looking distressed.

"I don't like to think of my sister – being trapped here," she mumbled.

"We shall pray for her, Miss Morris," Mr. Bramley assured her "and I am sure that all will be well.

"And as for you, Miss Hartnell, let's hope that there will be no more manifestations like this as I don't wish you to be upset in any way after you have been so poorly."

Aurora thanked him for his kindness and went back upstairs to her bedroom deep in thought.

Phyllis was tidying the room, arranging the few odd clothes Aurora had brought with her in the wardrobe.

"A penny for your thoughts, miss," she asked, as Aurora sat down by the fire that burned in the little grate.

Aurora told her about how Emily had appeared to her in the parlour and her meeting with Mr. Bramley.

"He says we should pray for Emily and, of course, I will do so. But what should I do if I see her again? She is so very sad – "

Phyllis sat down looking very serious.

"There be all manner of strange things in this old world, especially here in the West Country, that cannot be accounted for, and I'm sure if she does come to you again, Miss Aurora, you will know just what to do."

Aurora smiled.

"Thank you Phyllis, I am sure you are right, that is just what Mama would have said."

She paused for a moment to gaze out of the window at the garden, which was still bathed in winter sunlight.

"What day is it, Phyllis?" she asked. "I have lost all count of time, what with being ill."

"It be the sixth of January today, miss, the last day of Christmas."

Aurora sat back and recounted all the extraordinary things that had happened to her since her return home on Christmas Eve.

And now the New Year was already six days old, and there was no knowing what the coming months might bring.

She thought of the Earl, recalling how animated and happy he had appeared as he rode with them to Hadleigh Hall through the snow.

And the thrill that had run over her body when he had invited her to dine with him.

Could it really be the case that she would never feel that wonderful sensation ever again?

*

That evening after dinner was over, Aurora offered to help Miss Morris take down the bunches and garlands of greenery that had been hung up all around the house since the Christmas festivities.

It was easier for her, being younger and more agile, to reach the higher decorations.

As she balanced on a stool and reached up over the fireguard to take down a long festoon of holly and ivy from the mantelpiece in the parlour, she heard a small rustle, like a silk petticoat brushing over the floorboards, coming from behind her.

Her heart leapt in her breast and in her alarm she pricked her finger on a sharp holly leaf.

The air had suddenly turned cold in the parlour in spite of the logs burning brightly in the hearth.

She turned round very slowly and there behind her just a few yards away stood Emily in her grey dress.

Her face was white and there were deep caverns of shadow under her eyes.

Aurora noticed that her fine fair was escaping from the neat loops tucked over her ears and was hanging down in soft wisps.

"Emily," she said, breathing deeply to calm herself. "How are you, dear Emily?"

"He will not come – I wait for him, but – my love will not come – " came the jerky whispered reply although Emily's delicate lips did not move.

Aurora felt herself growing faint again, as the pain around her heart intensified.

'Mama! Help me,' she prayed silently speaking the words inside her head. 'What shall I do now?'

Aurora's face and hands grew warm and the pain in her heart lessened, as suddenly she knew what she had to say.

"Emily, dear Emily, he *cannot* come to you, for he is dead."

The figure in front of her bent forward and clutched her head in its hands and Aurora felt herself growing faint again, as a great wave of misery passed over her.

She quickly stepped off the stool in case she fell.

"But Emily," Aurora continued bravely, "you need not wait here for him, for he is waiting for you. It is safe now for you to move on from this house, so that you can join your Frederick in Heaven, where you can be together with him for ever."

Emily raised her ghostly head and stared at Aurora, a terrible light of grief and madness shining out of her pale eyes.

"Who are you to say this to me?" she seemed to be saying. "Where is your love? Are not you – too – waiting for one who will not come? Why should I believe you?"

Aurora felt faint and weak again and clutched at the metal of the fireguard behind her for support.

'I cannot do this,' she told herself, 'it is too hard.'

She really longed to feel the comfort of the loving presence of her Mama beside her, as she had done so many times before, but nothing came and so there was nothing to protect her from the terrible pain in the eyes of the woman who stood before her.

Suddenly it was as if a bolt of lightning had passed through her body, she seemed to see the Earl, standing in the great courtyard of Linford Castle, looking up at her in the Governess cart.

His eyes were shining and he spoke her name.

"*Miss Hartnell!*" he called out to her, "*I hope it will not be too long before we meet again.*"

Her heart was flooded with a great wave of joy and she turned back to the pale ethereal Emily, who now stood with her head hanging low and whose image seemed to be fading as the fire died down.

"You must believe me, Emily" she cried. "My love may never come, but while I live, I will still love him.

"And if it were possible for me to go to him and if he would have me, I would do so.

"*For it is Love that matters.* Love is the only thing, Emily! Go to your beloved Frederick and be together and love him for ever."

Emily's eyes glowed and her pale face broke into a smile.

She reached out a ghostly hand to Aurora not quite touching her and then suddenly the parlour was filled with soft light, as if all the candle flames had grown tall.

And then she was gone.

Aurora collapsed onto the sofa her limbs trembling.

The image of the Earl had been so vivid, it was as if he had been right there beside her.

And yet now he was gone again, leaving her once more alone.

In her heart she knew that Emily was now at peace, and had moved on to the realm of Divine Love.

No longer would her sad presence ever trouble the peaceful household at Treworra.

But what would become of her, Aurora?

Would her love ever come to her or would she ever be able to go to him?

Or would she remain here forever, a lonely spinster like Emily always looking back to what might have been?

CHAPTER TEN

"Mr. Bramley will be calling later this morning," announced Miss Morris, as she presided over the breakfast table at Treworra House three weeks after Aurora had had her final encounter with the ghostly Emily.

"I hope you do not mind, my dear?"

Miss Morris's pale cheeks glowed with a flattering rosy tint as she bent over the teapot.

She had been very cheerful over the last few days.

"Of course I should not mind," replied Aurora. "It will be delightful to have his company."

"The duties of a Parish Priest can be most arduous," continued Miss Morris, "forever helping the parishioners bear their burdens of poverty and bereavement and all the other ills that plague mankind. We must help to lighten the load whenever we can."

She blushed an even darker pink as she poured out a cup of tea for Aurora.

"Since you have come here, Aurora, you have made me see the importance of good companionship. You have brought a bright and joyful atmosphere into this house and I scarcely know myself for the quiet retiring creature that I used to be."

Aurora drank her tea hastily, wondering what Miss Morris might be about to say next, but the older woman sat back in her chair with a little smile on her face and stared happily out of the window.

After all the breakfast plates had been cleared away they moved to sit by the fire in the parlour and before too long a loud rat-a-tat was heard at the front door.

It was, of course, Mr. Bramley, who came in with a broad smile on his kindly red face.

"My dear Daphne, my dear Miss Hartnell," he said, bowing politely before taking a seat upon a large armchair near to Miss Morris, who was perched on the sofa.

'Daphne?' mused Aurora, 'I am sure he did call her by her Christian name before.'

Suddenly she felt her heart give a little flutter with a premonition of what was about to come.

"Have you yet told our dear young friend about our news?" Mr. Bramley said, turning to Miss Morris, his little blue eyes shining, but she shook her head and looked down at her sewing.

Mr. Bramley turned back to Aurora.

"I have sent to Dorset for my dear cousin Arthur, as I am in need of his services – for Miss Morris and I are to be married!"

Miss Morris made a sort of hiccoughing noise and dropped her sewing which she left lying on the floor as Mr. Bramley had now joined her on the sofa and was clasping both her hands in his.

"And I shall have the finest, dearest and sweetest wife that any man could wish for."

Miss Morris was overcome with emotion and could not speak.

Aurora felt her eyes welling up as she looked across at the sofa and saw the true and tender affection that shone from the eyes of both of them.

She wished them her most sincere congratulations and stood up, feeling that they might wish to be left alone.

"Thank you, my dear. I am sure that our happiness is in no small part due to you, Miss Hartnell. You seem to have worked some magic on this house, as I have cared for Daphne since first I knew her and yet it is only now that I have felt able to speak to her."

"And I am most truly blessed," sighed Miss Morris, with a catch in her voice, "as I have also cared for you, my dear Mr. Bramley, yet never could I have believed in this happiness you bring me."

Aurora smiled at them and made a hasty exit from the parlour, as with each passing minute she felt that her presence was superfluous.

She ran up the stairs to her room, suddenly feeling unaccountably sad.

It was delightful to see them so deliciously happy and yet she just could not help but feel even more alone and bereft of love herself.

Phyllis was there, sitting by the fire in her room and mending silk stockings.

She looked up when Aurora entered, but did not say anything.

"Miss Morris and Mr. Bramley are going to be wed, Phyllis. What do you think of that?"

Phyllis shook her head and tutted, carrying on with her sewing.

"Are you all right, Phyllis? You seem to have been very quiet of late."

Phyllis sighed.

"I am very happy for them, to be sure, Miss Aurora, for two nicer people I could not wish to meet. But what about us two spinsters? When shall *we* be wed?"

Phyllis looked so comically sad that Aurora found herself wanting to laugh, but she could not hurt her maid's feelings.

"I am so sorry," she said instead, "I did not realise you felt like that."

"I did hope," sighed Phyllis, "that when you helped that poor sad woman, Emily, to move on to the other side, takin' all her grief and misery with her, that things might start to work out a bit for us – "

Aurora sighed as well and then she shivered as she suddenly remembered Lord Moreton's rough hands forcing the emeralds around her neck.

"You know, Phyllis, I think being a spinster may be far more pleasant than being married to someone you don't like!"

"That's all very well for you to say, Miss Aurora, for you have many years of your youth ahead of you."

Phyllis stabbed her needle into the stocking she was darning.

"But surely it is not too late for you. You are not so old, Phyllis, you could not marry and have a family too if you wished."

"It be a near thing," mumbled Phyllis and then she suddenly smiled, "but if truth be told, I would find it hard to up and leave you after all these years."

Aurora was pleased to see her maid more cheerful, as she knew that since they had been in Cornwall, Phyllis had been to visit some of her brothers and sisters.

And it had been hard for her to see them with their own young families growing up, while she had devoted all the best years of her life to Aurora and her mother.

She sat down on the little sofa and looked out over the garden, but even the sight of a large flock of small birds playing in the trees could not lift her spirits.

It was all very well for Phyllis to tell her that she was young and had plenty of time ahead of her, but the heavy sadness that filled her heart told her that she would never be able to marry.

'I have met the one man I could love,' she mused, 'and he despises me – because he believes I have promised myself to another man. And even if I had turned my back on Lord Moreton, the Earl would still think badly of me, as I would have broken my word.'

There was nothing for it but to accept her situation with good grace and to give her every support and blessing to the kindly Miss Morris and her husband-to-be.

*

Over the next few days Aurora had her work cut out, as Miss Morris was thrown into a panic at the idea of her impending wedding and had no idea of how a bride-to-be should behave.

She was determined to be married in her old grey Sunday dress and it took all Aurora's patience to persuade her that it would be proper and fitting for her to wear a wedding gown.

Miss Morris finally agreed to a modestly cut satin wedding dress.

"But it must be in grey," she persisted, alarmed by Aurora's suggestion of cream or ivory as possible colours, "Pale grey, if you insist, but I do not want to look anything out of the ordinary."

"But it's *your* day," urged Aurora, "and everyone will be expecting you to look lovely."

But Miss Morris simply blushed and looked most uncomfortable.

So it was left to Aurora and Phyllis to arrange with the local dressmaker to make the simple elegant dress.

Aurora offered to trim the dress herself, and several days later she was sitting in the parlour, sewing small silk flowers onto the sleeves of the gown, when she heard an unfamiliar knock at the door.

'Who can that possibly be?' she wondered, 'it is not Mr. Bramley as he always raps three times.'

Miss Morris came hurrying into the parlour.

"Aurora. You have a visitor. *A gentleman!*"

Aurora jumped to her feet, spilling silk flowers all over the carpet and the armchairs.

It must be Lord Moreton!

Somehow he had been able to find her.

Maybe he had discovered the necklace or traced his two coach horses to this remote part of Cornwall.

"No!" she exclaimed, "I cannot see him – "

But she was too late.

A tall figure was now striding through the door and approaching her, blocking out the light from the window as he stood before her.

"Miss Hartnell," came a deep resonant voice.

It was the Earl.

Aurora sat right down again, her legs trembling and her breath catching in her throat.

She clutched the grey silk gown to her.

Where was Miss Morris?

Why had she not stayed in the parlour?

"I must speak with you," the Earl began in a cold flat voice.

Aurora looked up at him for a second and saw that his dark eyes were as dull and hard as stones.

'Truly,' she told herself, 'he despises me for all the light and joy has vanished from his face.'

"Whatever that strange piece of frippery is that you

are clutching – it will be ruined," he commented, a sharp note of impatience in his voice.

"Oh!"

Aurora looked down and saw that the grey silk was being badly creased as she twisted it in her hands.

"It is Miss Morris's wedding dress!"

She could not believe how cold and harsh the Earl sounded, and how different he now seemed from the man she remembered so incredibly well – the courteous, lively and handsome gentleman riding with her through the snow.

"Ah, the wedding," sighed the Earl, "the fortuitous wedding – without which I should never have found you."

"Mr. – Bramley's cousin – " stammered Aurora.

"Yes, indeed, my chaplain. He has told me that you were here at Treworra House."

Aurora glanced at him again, but the Earl was now looking down at the carpet.

"I have some news for you, Miss Hartnell. Perhaps I may be seated?"

"Of course."

Aurora hastened to clear away the silk flowers from the armchair opposite her and the Earl sat down.

"I have come directly from Hadleigh Hall, where I have seen your father."

"*Papa!*" cried Aurora, suddenly fearful.

"He is very sick and the doctors hold out little hope that he will live beyond the month."

Aurora gasped and tried to hold back the tears that began to spill down her cheeks.

"I do wish I could go to him," she whispered, "poor Papa."

The Earl stood up again and began to pace up and down the parlour.

"This is why I have come for you," he continued. "Your stepmother has gone!"

"*Gone*?" echoed Aurora.

"She is in Monte Carlo,"

The Earl ran a hand through his dark hair,

"With your fiancé, Lord Moreton!"

"But – how? How did this happen?" asked Aurora, her heart pounding.

"After you abandoned him, Lord Moreton went to his house in London –

The Earl looked away from her as he continued to pace up and down,

"And, in the manner of one heartbroken, he took to playing at cards. He then struck very lucky and with his winnings, he has gone off and *eloped* to the Continent with Lady Hartnell."

Aurora dropped the wedding dress and pressed her hands against her cheeks.

"*I don't believe you!*"

"He is apparently well known in London Society as a gambler," the Earl then added and she detected a flash of scorn in his dark eyes.

Aurora breathed deeply, trying to calm herself.

"Why, I must go to Papa! I must be with him."

The Earl was looking at her gravely and she flushed as she felt the intensity of his stare.

"He needs you, Miss Hartnell, and my carriage will be here directly to take you to Hadleigh Hall."

His lips twisted in a wry smile.

"But what of your betrothed, Lord Moreton? Do you feel nothing at his desertion?"

Aurora felt her face turn fiery red with shame and embarrassment and she wished that the parlour floor would open up and swallow her.

"Perhaps I am speaking out of turn," the Earl added sarcastically, "as this is clearly a matter of some delicacy."

He moved towards the door.

"My compliments to you, Miss Hartnell. As I have indicated my carriage is at your disposal and I suggest that you leave at your earliest convenience."

And then he was gone, leaving Aurora trembling on the sofa.

'I must try to collect myself,' she determined as she gathered up the wedding dress tenderly, collecting all the little silk flowers.

'How strange that he should find me here, like this, working on another woman's wedding dress.'

Then she thought of the hard cold way that the Earl had looked at her and the tears she had been trying to hold back slid down her cheeks.

'He thinks the worst of me. He believes me to be fickle and dishonest. And yet he came all this way to find me and to tell me about Papa's illness!'

Aurora sprang to her feet and ran to the front door.

The Earl was standing by the garden gate, looking out over the green fields, as he waited for his mount.

She ran to his side, her face hot with shyness.

"Thank you very much, my Lord," she struggled to keep her voice calm, "for coming to tell me about Papa's illness and for offering me your carriage. I am most deeply grateful to you."

The Earl started, as he had not heard her coming up behind him and then he looked down at her.

"It is all my pleasure, although perhaps you would rather abandon the carriage and take one of my horses, as from what I have heard, I think it might suit you better to make the journey at a wild gallop!"

And suddenly he smiled at her and his eyes shone with life and humour just as she remembered him.

Aurora bit her lip and did not know where to look, as there was such pain and confusion in her heart that she almost thought she would faint.

The Earl reached down and took her hand and she felt her whole body thrill at his warm touch.

"I wish you a safe journey, Miss Hartnell," he said, still smiling, "but I would advise you to make use of my carriage."

Aurora could not speak, but she nodded, and then looked up, meeting his dark gaze for a second.

As they both looked into each other's eyes, she felt a strange sensation pass through her.

It was as if she was gazing into the eyes of someone most dear and familiar to her, someone she had known for all of her life and for all Eternity.

And then he released her hand, as Miss Morris's groom was approaching with the Earl's horse and Aurora watched him leap into the saddle and race away across the fields.

*

From time to time throughout the carriage journey back to Hadleigh Hall, Aurora felt again the sensation she had experienced when the Earl had taken her hand.

She knew that she was sitting upon the same velvet cushions he had rested on and was looking out through the same window that he must have gazed out of many times.

But in spite of this comfort, her heart was torn with

fear and anxiety for her poor Papa and their slow lurching journey over muddy roads seemed interminable.

At last they were there and as the wheels crunched over the gravel drive, Aurora sprang down from the Earl's carriage, deeply relieved to see that her father's bedroom window was aglow with candlelight.

'He is still with us,' she whispered to herself, as she ran up the wide staircase, untying her bonnet and flinging it aside as she ran.

Her father seemed to have grown even thinner and paler over the few weeks she had been away.

His shrunken frame was propped up on a mountain of soft feather pillows and every breath he took seemed to cause him great difficulty.

"Papa," murmured Aurora, falling to her knees and taking his fragile bony hand in hers.

"Marianne," he grunted, "is it you?"

Aurora felt a tear slip down her cheek.

"Papa, it is not dear Mama, it is me, Aurora. I have come home to look after you."

His pale eyes blinked at her and then he sighed as if in relief.

Aurora felt his grip tighten round her hand and next he fell back on the pillows and seemed to sleep.

*

For seven days and nights Aurora remained at her father's side.

The doctor came, stout and severe in his long black coat, and informed her gravely that Lord Hartnell was very sick with pneumonia and without constant care and love he might never recover.

"It is a great killer of the elderly," he intoned after

spending a good deal of time at Lord Hartnell's bedside, "and of those who believe they are alone in the world."

"Papa, you are not alone," Aurora whispered after the doctor had left, "for I am with you and will never leave you."

After a week of agonised watching and waiting, he seemed to improve somewhat, his breathing became easier and he expressed a desire for beef tea.

Aurora ordered some immediately from the kitchen and fed him gently from a spoon, as if he was a baby.

Then she settled him back against his pillows.

Her head was swimming with tiredness, as she had scarcely dared to sleep herself since she had arrived back at Hadleigh Hall.

"Miss Aurora, you need some rest," urged Phyllis, touching her shoulder gently. "I will watch your father for you and call you if you are wanted for anythin'."

Aurora thought longingly of her soft feather bed.

But then she noticed that the sun was shining over the Park and she realised that she had not been out of doors since she had arrived back at Hadleigh Hall.

She then made her way onto the terrace and stood basking in the spring sunlight, listening to the birds singing as they flitted from branch to branch in the trees.

Aurora had no idea how long she had been standing there, breathing the sweet air and feeling the warm sun on her cheeks.

Suddenly she heard the crunch of a footstep behind her and saw a long shadow fall on the terrace beside her.

"You are lost in a reverie, Miss Hartnell," came a familiar deep voice.

It was the Earl's, and she turned to find that he was standing so close beside her that she could feel the warmth from his body.

"I am so happy," she warbled, afraid to look up at him and desperately trying to control her voice, which was trembling, "because I think Papa is getting better at last."

The Earl took her hands and turned her to face him.

Aurora felt herself filling with a wild sweet fire, so that her soul wanted to sing out in ecstasy just like one of the songbirds that flocked through the trees.

"You have not left his side for days," the Earl was saying. "I have come many times to try and speak to you, but you were always with him."

Aurora suddenly felt confusion and fear wash over her, as her sensations were so strong and like nothing she had ever experienced before.

She raised her head and met the Earl's dark eyes, looking deep into them and the fear vanished as once again she felt that this man was so familiar to her and that she was safe with him.

"Your sweetness, your kindness and your integrity have put me to shame, Miss Hartnell."

Aurora felt his hands on her shoulders drawing her to him and then the fire inside her grew stronger and more insistent.

The Earl was still speaking to her urgently and his words seemed to be tumbling over themselves.

"I have just recently discovered the truth about your stepmother," he whispered, his breath caressing Aurora's ear as softly as a feather.

"She feared that your Papa would die and leave his estate to you. And so she plotted to marry you off to her erstwhile lover, Lord Moreton, so that you couldn't inherit Hadleigh Hall and it would all go to her.

"And so when you foiled her little plot by running away and when Moreton came into some money, she took up with him again and fled to Monte Carlo, where I pray they may gamble all his ill-gotten gains away!"

Aurora gasped with horror and her eyes filled with hot tears that spilled over and ran down her cheeks as she dwelt on what might have happened if she and Phyllis had not been able to outwit Lord Moreton.

"Don't weep," the Earl tried to sooth her. "Sweet one, you are safe now."

"But – if you had not stopped the carriage on the road – "

Aurora found herself shaking, remembering all the horror of that terrible rain-drenched encounter.

The Earl bent and touched his lips to Aurora's wet cheeks.

Her legs began to give way beneath her at the sweet sensation, but he caught her tightly in his arms.

"Please forgive me," he breathed, his voice growing deeper with the intensity of passion, "how could I have left you there with him on that fearsome night?

"But I was angry with you, so incredibly angry that you had let me down. And then he said that you were his *betrothed*!"

"No, it was a terrible mistake, a misunderstanding."

She was about to try to explain it all again, when her words were silenced as the Earl fastened his lips on hers in a tender but burning kiss.

Aurora felt her soul flying to meet his.

And then she could feel both of them melt into one with all the sweetness and burgeoning life of the glorious spring day around them.

She drank his kiss into the very depths of her being.

"From the first moment I met you," the Earl was saying as he broke off from the kiss and leant his face next to hers, "I loved you. I wanted you near me. I could not bear to think of you with another."

"I was never, never – " Aurora began, but the Earl grasped her arms in his hands and held her away from him so he could see her face.

"Please, Miss Hartnell, *will you be my wife?*"

The Earl stood before her and she saw for a second a great vulnerability in his dark eyes, as he continued,

"Will you stay by my side for the rest of our lives and never leave me?"

"For Eternity, I will be with you," she whispered, and closed her eyes, almost fainting as he bent to kiss her again.

The short spring day was ending and the light was beginning to fade, as they made their way back to the Hall.

The Earl held Aurora's hand tightly in his as she explained that she could not yet leave her Papa, until she was sure that he was truly well again.

"I will wait for you, my darling," he said, drawing her to him, and she felt his deep voice vibrate through her being, "for as long as you wish."

"My heart is in your keeping, my time is yours to command, my Lord."

And Aurora turned to him, as they stood outside the front door of Hadleigh Hall and felt again the timeless and Heavenly blessing of his passionate lips on hers.

*

Lord Hartnell seemed to gain strength as the days grew longer and it was just a few weeks later that he was well enough to be wrapped up and carried to his carriage for the short journey to Linford Castle.

The clouds of daffodils and primroses that grew in little clumps in the courtyard raised their glowing heads to the sun.

In the Castle's Chapel the light poured in through the windows in fountains of vivid colour.

These drew flashing sparkles from the tiny crystals and pearls that covered nearly all the glorious white gown of the young girl who had just become a wife.

Aurora stood very still, happiness flooding through her heart as her body tingled with excitement.

She gazed at the smooth golden band on her finger.

She did not need to look at the tall handsome man, *her husband*, who stood beside her.

With every nerve in her body she felt his presence and his love, filling her with the sweet fire of passion and yet holding her safe.

The Earl's Chaplain, Mr. Bramley's cousin, Arthur, who had only just returned from performing the nuptials of Miss Morris in Cornwall, was still speaking.

Aurora smiled as she peered over her shoulder at the altar where another marriage was taking place.

A tall red-headed man, swathed in a fine tartan kilt that revealed his splendid muscular legs, stood there, and, at his side, a small dark-haired woman in a demure pearl-coloured dress and veil.

"What is it, my dear love?" the Earl asked softly.

"I am just so happy," murmured Aurora, "as clever Phyllis has found a way to stay with me *and* be married to a man she loves."

The Earl laughed.

"She has had her eye on my Duncan from the very beginning, I think, and I could not wish her a finer match."

He took Aurora by the hand and led her out into the courtyard, where a group of local musicians were playing on fiddles and pipes.

Lord Hartnell was there, comfortably tucked into a large wheelchair and he smiled and raised his thin hand to the two of them, his old blue eyes shining with happiness.

The Earl waved back and then turned to Aurora and looked her up and down, his eyes shining.

"Your wedding dress is so very perfect," he sighed, "for, like you, it is as pure and as beautiful as the sunshine falling on a field of snow."

Aurora's heart swelled as she remembered looking out over the Park at Hadleigh Hall after the snowstorm and seeing it shining like a field of tiny diamonds.

She knew that her Mama had been beside her then and perhaps had even known of this incredible happiness that awaited her.

"But now, my darling wife," the Earl was saying, "surely it is my turn for you to work your magic upon my home. I think you promised me once that you would lift the sadness that has always plagued this place, just as I know you did at Valley Farm and at Treworra House."

Aurora looked around the courtyard at the flowers and the happy smiling faces –

And at gracious old Linford Castle, which had been festooned with blossoms and greenery for their wedding.

She could not see darkness anywhere or feel any sadness.

Instead, with a shock of delight, she seemed to hear the happy voices of children and thought she saw a troop of little ones running out of the door of the Castle to play in the courtyard.

"There is no need," she breathed. "For there is so much Love here that all the sadness has fled.

"There is nothing here, I can certainly assure you, my wonderful husband, but happiness, beauty and joy.

"Surely this must be *a Heaven on Earth*!"

The Earl caught her in his arms and spun her round, her white skirts billowing out like the petals of a flower, as her heart lifted to join his in an ecstasy of Love.

For all Eternity and beyond for ever.